Travel With Me Through Time

Theodore Aguilera

Theodore Aguilera

Dedicated to
My Mother and Father

Travel With Me Through Time

© 2010 Theodore Aguilera
All rights Reserved.

Published by Dosey Books
El Sobrante, California, U.S.A.

ISBN: 978-0-615-35535-1

Contents

Chapter 1:   *A Day Like Any Other*   1

Chapter 2:   *The Time Machine*   9

Chapter 3:   *Tombstone*   29

Chapter 4:   *Gunnar's Future*   45

Chapter 5:   *A Rose In 1956*   51

Chapter 6:   *Gunnar's Past*   61

Chapter 7:   *Gunnar's Present*   67

Chapter 8:   *The Time Planet*   73

Chapter 9:   *A Matter of Money*   103

Chapter 10:   *Out of Time*   129

Chapter 11:   *Rescuing Friends*   145

Chapter 12:   *Gunnar, Egyptologist*   155

Chapter 13:   *Getting Away From It All*   163

Chapter 14:   *The Men on The Moon*   175

Chapter 15:   *Crossroads*   185

Theodore Aguilera

Chapter 1: **A Day Like Any Other**

I wake up early this morning.

Going downstairs, I see my older brother, James, having a cup of coffee in the kitchen and reading today's paper in t-shirt and jeans.

Our house is unusual. Three stories high, it is shaped like a dome. This *is* California—just across the Bay from San Francisco.

"Morning, Gunnar," James says. "What's the plan this morning?"

"I'm going to head downtown and get something to eat. The Sun's up and it looks like a good day for a walk."

"If you like to walk, I guess."

"Yesterday," he continues, "I saw this woman down the street that would have knocked your socks off!"

"Well, you'd know better than anyone—with all those women you get to take pictures of in the city," I remark.

"Yeah, but there, women are just work, not people. They're there to do a job and make a living, like me. I can even touch their legs—or any other part of their body—to get a better picture and it's okay. It's just part of the job. It means big money to those businesses I work for. But when the work's done, they become women again and sometimes we get together at the bar across the street and have a good time."

"Well, I'll see you later, brother," I tell him.

As I walk out of the house, I do not know that up ahead are things that will change my life forever, just waiting to happen with no way of stopping them.

Walking down the same streets I always travel, I see a very lovely young lady going by. Maybe this is the one James was talking about. She's in a blue shirt and tight-fitting jeans. I can't take my eyes off of her! She knows it, too. Women know men are always looking at them. She gives me a big smile.

That brightens up my day. I will not forget that smile on the face that God gave her. It's nice to see a pretty smile in this world of ours.

1

There's another one! Today is my lucky day. This lovely lady is washing her sports car in a white t-shirt and shorts. Bare footed! I like to see a woman without shoes—it's sexy to me. And she has a face so sweet and kind that no man could forget. I could get lost in those baby blue eyes. Oh, and her long, light brown hair is blowing in the wind. I'd pay for what I'm seeing now. All I need is a cold beer and a chair.

"Hi there," I say. "It's a nice day today for washing your car."

She looks over and replies, "Yes, the Sun's up and it's a hot and wonderful day with the water to cool me off."

I've been a girl-watcher a long time now. With my sunglasses on, I can look at all the pretty women I want and they can't see my eyes. The guy who invented sunglasses must have been a girl-watcher, too.

To my surprise, she calls me back. "You live by here, don't you?"

"Yes, I'm close by. You know that dome house on Hilltop Drive? I live there with my brother, James. We've lived there a long time but I haven't seen you here before."

"That's a big house for just you and your brother," she comments. "I always loved that house. I always wanted to see it from the inside."

"Well, anytime you want, just come over for a chat. Our door will always be open for a pretty lady like yourself. We have the occasional party, too, and you're always welcome."

"Okay then, bye" she says.

I smile and continue walking on.

A little farther up the road, I see my favorite restaurant.

It looks very crowded through the window. Should I go in or not? They do have good food and are very nice people. The atmosphere is good, too. Teenagers like to come and listen to music and even dance.

I walk in and look around at all the people crammed in this place. I see some customers getting up from a booth. That was good timing. I sit myself in the booth, make myself at home and wait to be served.

I see yet another attractive lady seated all by herself nearby.

Today really is my lucky day! Three beauties so far!

She looks right at me.

She has two of the most beautiful eyes I have ever seen. I just love a woman's eyes—don't ask me why—but it's the first thing I notice. They talk to me and tell me about her.

She's wearing my favorite color on a dress, too—red.

Women know how to dress and to get a man's attention. And this one's good at it and she knows it. God, have mercy! I'm only human.

However, having her eyes on me does make me a little nervous.

Now she's touching her long, black hair. I can feel it from here.

The way she keeps looking at me—I wish I were there next to her, holding her hand in mine. To be with a lady like her—that shouldn't be too much to ask for. I know she wants me there. I can feel it…

She gives me a wink.

I'm going over there and I'm going to talk to her right now!

As I rise, a man walks in and goes straight to her table. He gives her a big kiss on those nice lips that could have been mine and sits beside her. She starts talking to him as she should be talking to me.

I guess she has someone already. Damn.

I sit back in my seat, alone.

Maybe next time I'll get lucky.

She sits there talking to the man but keeps looking over at me with those eyes of hers. A woman like that can get a man into big trouble.

The waiter finally comes to my table. He's dressed in black pants and a white shirt. "Can I take your order, sir?"

"Yes. It's a little busy in here today, heh?"

"It's this way most of the time. You know that, don't you? I have seen you in here before—I am right, sir?"

"Yes, I've been here many times. You do have good food. I would like a burger with fries and a glass of water with lots of ice."

"Fine, I'll be back with your order shortly."

"Thank you."

I look around and see a young man pushing a cart filled with dirty dishes walking toward my table. He looks a little wild to me with his long red and blue hair. He has funny clothes, too, with holes in them.

3

He comes and cleans my table while listening to some kind of music. Half-dancing to it, he asks, "How's it going, man?"

"It's going okay."

He finishes with my table and moves on to the next, bouncing to his music the whole time. He looks about as happy as a man can be, doing his job cleaning tables.

Another man walks into the restaurant.

He looks around as though he's looking for someone.

He seems very out of place, dressed like a cowboy you would see on TV with a big white cowboy hat.

He looks right at me as if he knows me somehow and approaches with a big smile on his face.

I think to myself, "Why is he looking at me like that?" Yet, seeing him for the first time, deep down I feel as though I will know this man but do not know how. I do have a little ESP.

Others look at him strangely.

He walks to my table and asks if he can sit with me, since all of the other tables are full. Sitting alone, I politely agree.

"Thanks" he says as he takes his seat. "Nice town you have here. You do live here, don't you?"

"I live here but I was born in Texas, if you must know."

He reaches up and touches his hat, lifting it up a little. "You have a lot of good people who live here in this town of yours."

"Sure. But nice people live all over this world of ours."

"That's true," he says. "By the way, what's your name?"

"Gunnar Best. And you are?"

"Jack" he says as he touches his hat once again.

The waiter arrives with my food. He looks at me and then at Jack, the cowboy. "Oh—can I take your order while I'm here, sir?"

"I'll just have a cup of coffee for now, thank you."

"I'll be right back with that."

"So, Jack, where do you call home?"

4

I'm all over this world of ours. Wherever I hang my hat is where I call home. Today it's your town, but tomorrow, only God knows... Traveling has been good for me, always new places to see—nobody would believe the things I've seen. I met so many good people over the years out there, too. Some are dead now, but to me, they still live. They lived good lives when they were alive, anyway.

"What about you, Gunnar? Travel much?"

"No. Too expensive. Can't afford it right now but maybe someday in the future. I'm just too poor, I guess."

The waiter arrives with Jack's coffee. "Is everything okay here?"

"Yes, everything's fine, thank you," I tell him.

Jack leans forward. As I chew on my burger and fries, he asks, "What do you think about *time,* Gunnar?"

"Well, at eight o'clock I'll be home having my dinner. At eleven o'clock I'll be sleeping like a baby."

"That's not what I'm talking about. I'm talking about *time travel.* Do you believe a man can go into the future and the past?"

"I believe it's possible..."

"Why do you think it's possible, Gunnar?"

"Well, the bible contains *The Book of Revelation.* In it, John wrote about things that will come to be on the very last days of our times. Therefore, he must have seen the future or been there himself. So did Isaiah, Ezekiel and Jeremiah."

"Yes, but why can't we travel to the future right now?" he asks.

"We don't have the technology. I believe we will someday but not in our lifetime. We will be able to see the future and things long gone. We'll see them just as if they were right here today.

"Why do you ask?"

"Would you believe me if I told you that yesterday I was drinking beer with a pretty young woman in 1914? It was a long time ago but it was like yesterday to me. We were laughing and having a great time together—if you know what I mean... If you were there you would've had a good time, too."

5

"Did I hear you right—you were in 1914, yesterday?"

"That's what I said. Do you have wax in your ears?"

I pause to finish my french fry and collect my thoughts. "Well, my mother always said to me, "Never call a man a liar until he shows you why he said that."

"Well, believe me or not, it's the truth.

"You have a watch, don't you?"

"Yeah, why?" I ask.

"Unless you've gone through time yourself, you don't know the first thing about it. To you, time is just the hour hand and the minute hand and that's it. But me, I can actually *stop* time if I want to."

"Not you or anybody else can do that," I tell him.

"One of the women in 1914 is named Candy—and I like her a lot. She's been really nice to me for several years. I see her now and then, whenever I can. In 1914, women think differently from women today. I have a good time with her when I'm there. Some good beer, too.

"Sometimes I think about bringing her here to our time. But I care for her and know it would be wrong to do that to her. She belongs in the past. This time belongs to us."

He then pauses and looks directly at me. "One day, you will have to make that decision, too. Don't do it. It can change history."

"I'm not sure what you're talking about," I respond.

"Beer only costs ten cents a bottle then!"

"Why are you telling me about changing history?"

"Things change from one minute to another, Gunnar. You should know what to do when it comes up. Now you know.

"It was good beer, too, for ten cents a bottle!

"You'd like it there in the past. The women are so beautiful—not like the women in our time. Beautiful women, without all that makeup on their faces. Natural, like God wants them to be."

"May I ask, how do you do it—go back in time?"

"Let me show you outside. I have a machine—it's a *time machine*. It can take you to the past or to the future—anywhere you want to go in time. I like 1914 'cause the beer is good and cheap. The women are not bad either, as I said."

While finishing up my food, I think to myself that this man sitting across from me sounds a little crazy in the head. On the other hand, he could be telling the truth.

"Okay, I want to see this time machine of yours."

At that point, the young man who cleaned my table drops some dishes on the floor. Jack springs up and spins around quickly. Acting as if he had drawn a gun from a holster, he extends his empty hand. With an embarrassed look, he mutters to me, "Sorry for that."

"Its okay, Jack. I can live with it."

Others, however, look at him as if he were insane. Perhaps he is. Maybe I'm a little crazy too.

Chapter 2: **The Time Machine**

Finished with my lunch, we head out now to take a look at Jack's so-called "time machine."

As we depart, I look back to that woman who was checking me out earlier. The man she was with is gone. She blows me a subtle kiss. I give her a wink as I leave the restaurant with Jack.

"Over here, Gunnar—it's by this old oak tree. Can you see it?"

I walk over to where Jack is standing. I look around but do not see anything that looks like a time machine.

What is wrong with this guy? Is he just nutty in the head?

Again, Jack asks me to look around but I do not see a damn thing except for an old tree and a rock and some grass.

I turn to Jack and ask, "Are you playing some kind of joke on me? If you are, I've got better things to do than stare at trees and rocks."

"Then you should stand over here, Gunnar, and look around."

"There's nothing out here, Jack. Can't you see that?"

"Do you see the time machine now?" he asks.

"No, asshole! I do not see a damn thing! What is wrong with you? Do you need a head doctor or something? I feel like a fool out here!"

I'm about ready to go when he says, "I'll show you I'm not crazy. I was testing to see what kind of man you are based on your reaction. I do have a time machine. It's two feet from where you're standing."

"Well, seeing is believing."

Jack takes something out of his pocket and hands it to me. It kind of looks like two coins stuck on top of each other.

"What is this?"

"I call that a *revealer.* With it, you will see my time machine. You and I will be the only ones who can. Don't let go of it. If you do, you will not be able to move even your little finger or talk to me. You will be frozen like ice. Look over to there by the tree now."

A large gray craft now stands before me! It looks more like a UFO than a time machine. It's like a curved dish with windows all around.

It has no wheels but rests on the ground. Inside, it looks like a big cab with two red bucket seats. It has a dashboard with strange instruments on it. I have no idea what they do. There seems to be a steering wheel. Not like one you would see on a car, but more like on a plane.

"There it is," he says, "a time machine that can go into the future or the past or wherever you want. So now who's telling the truth and who's crazy? We know I'm not lying, so you must be the crazy one."

"I have no words to describe what I am seeing here," I respond.

It then comes to my notice that everything around us has stopped moving, just like he said. Every car stands motionless. People I have known my whole life appear frozen solid.

This makes me a little nervous.

"What is going on here?"

I see a woman who lives across the street from me. I run to her, grab her shoulders and shout, "Barbara, Barbara! Can you see me?" She feels like a piece of wood. I shake her but she does not react.

"What happened to them? They look almost dead."

"They're not. They just can't move because the time machine has been activated. They will soon return to normal as though nothing had ever happened to them. I did tell you in the restaurant that I could stop time, remember? Now you see for yourself."

The time machine then rises off the ground as wings extend from beneath it, as if ready to fly. It stops, though, a little off the ground as the doors slowly begin to open on either side.

Some kind of energy can be seen on its metal skin. It gives off a low light in different colors, all mixing together, getting brighter and brighter. I've never seen anything like this. What power it must have! You can actually see it. Maybe this makes it pass through time…

To the touch, it gives off a kind of static electric charge. It's a bit hot—like touching thousands of volts of electricity—although it does not hurt. The colors begin to rotate around the machine and my hand. I gaze upon its beauty. I will never forget it.

The craft is divided down the middle by two doors. Each of which has swung down to become a step on either side for climbing inside.

"Gunnar, do you want to travel with me through time to the past? Imagine us in 1914, having a beer. If not, I'll just find someone else."

"I would *love* to go with you to see the past. Who wouldn't?"

He smiles and gestures to get in. "Well then, 1914 here we come!"

Stepping onto the lowered door, I start to feel a bit nervous. After all, this is my first time in a time machine.

As we sit there, the doors slowly start to close by themselves.

Strangely, I feel this urge to get out and run back home where I belong but don't know how to say this to Jack.

"You okay there?" he asks. "A little scared?"

"I'm fine!"

The time machine shakes and begins lifting up off of the ground. This makes me more anxious. But as much as I want to get out of this, there's no turning back now as we begin ascending into the sky.

"Are you thirsty for that beer I promised you, Gunnar?"

"I could go for that and a couple more right now."

I am then reminded that we are about to visit 1914. This blows my mind! Stuff like this does not come along every day. To witness what my grandfather saw and heard back then and have beer with it too! To go through time itself—to see it and to touch it...

I notice that the time machine does not make any sound, as though it doesn't even have a motor.

Looking out the window, everything is returning back to a normal speed—except backwards.

"Ah! Is that why nobody can see or hear the time machine when we're in it?" I ask. "It's just in a different time from them?"

"That's right. We are always one second ahead."

Jack starts pulling the steering wheel back a bit further. The time machine begins slowly raising us even higher than before.

The days and nights start changing from one to another. They're going by so fast—like pages turning in a book. First, the Sun goes by then the Moon, like a ball being thrown around and around the Earth. I can't believe what I am seeing out this window! And I haven't even had a drop of alcohol today, either.

"Gunnar, you have a cell phone on you?"

"Yeah. Why?"

"Will you let me see it?"

I give him my phone and he places it within a compartment in the dashboard. He then pushes a button which activates a light. A moment later, it turns off. He pulls it out and hands it back to me.

"Here's your new cell phone. I hope you enjoy it."

"What just happened to it?"

"Well, now your phone can make calls to any other phone in the world, at any time you want it to. If you're in 1782, you can call a girlfriend in 2010 to tell her that you love her."

"Amazing."

It's quite roomy in here. The dashboard looks like the dashboard of an airplane. It has many knobs, lights and switches, but I have no idea what they do. In the middle is some type of computer.

"This will be a whole new world for you, Gunnar. For me, it is an old world for an old man of fifty. Good times await us."

He pushes his hat up and pulls the steering wheel back a bit more, then turns it a bit. The machine soars even higher into the sky.

The people below us are moving around like little ants as we find ourselves a lot higher now.

"Wow. How fast can this time machine of yours go?"

"It can go very fast or very slow. Five miles an hour or thousands of miles an hour."

I look out the window and can see the days going by even faster.

"As I told you before," he says, "I have been all over this world of ours from top to bottom. Traveling takes a lot of time. So you need to go very fast to get back again at the same time and place you left…"

Seeing danger, I quickly shout, "Look out for that brick building!"

"What's that you say?"

"We're going too fast!"

"Faster? Okay, if that's what you want!"

"No! Look out!"

"Oh, I see it! But it's too late! It's been nice knowing you…"

My fears quickly subside as we pass straight through the building and come out the other side.

Jack laughs. "To see your face—I love it! I heard you but we were in no danger at all."

"That wasn't funny. I saw my whole life flash before my eyes and you think it was a good joke—ha, ha, ha. What's wrong with you?"

"I'm sorry," he says with a big smile on his face.

His apology does not make me any less angry. "Fine, let's get to 1914 and get that damn beer. I really need a drink now."

As I look out the window, I see parents with their children playing on the grass below.

Jack pushes down on the steering wheel and turns it a little. The time machine slowly settles to the ground and stops. It then rises a bit off the ground but soon stops, allowing the doors to open and letting us step off. Everyone stops moving.

"This thing has *so* much power, it can stop time itself…" he says.

We climb out and the doors begin to close. It then returns to the ground as its wings retract under it and out of view. From there, the glow it gives off finally fades while the machine, itself, vanishes.

Everyone starts moving again. The children play as if nothing had happened.

We landed on a vacant lot.

Not far away, I see a big sign up ahead that says "Saloon".

"How about we have some fun here in this town," Jack says as we walk down the street. "Some good beer and good women—what more could a man ask for?"

As we work our way toward the saloon Jack asks, "So, what do you think of 1914?"

"It looks a little dirty to me, but it's okay."

I see papers on the ground along with some old cans and boxes. I don't think anybody will be picking up this garbage any time soon.

I then stop and remark, "Everything's in color."

"What do you mean?"

"Well, I've seen this time period in black and white on television but now it's in color here in real life."

Jack grins.

We walk for about a block until reaching the saloon. Looking at it, I think it needs a paint job pretty badly. This whole area is run-down. It could be the south end of town.

"You thirsty, Gunnar?"

"Yes, I'm very thirsty after your last joke, Jack. A beer or two will help me forget about that."

"Are you still holding that against me? It was just a joke."

"Yes sir, I'm still holding that against you."

"What can I do? It's already happened and we cannot change that. And the truth is that it was very funny, even if you don't think so."

"When you see your whole life end before your eyes and then find out it was a joke—that may be funny to you, but it's not to me."

"Okay, Gunnar, you win. Let's get some beer and forget about it. What I did won't happen again, you have my word."

We walk inside the saloon and over to the bar.

The bartender is a very fat, bald-headed man. His shirt was white at one time but is not anymore. His pants are filthy as well. He smells and it's obvious that he needs a bath real bad but doesn't know it. He must sleep in those clothes.

With a cigar in his mouth, he puts his hand on the bar and asks, "Can I help you men?"

Jack replies, "Yes, I'd like two of the best beers you got."

"That's gunna cost you twenty-five cents each. It's a bit high but it's real good beer and well worth it. That okay with you?"

"That will be fine. It's for my best friend here. I think he's worth about twenty-five cents. What about that, Gunnar?"

14

I shake my head slightly.

Jack says, "We'll take two, bartender."

The bartender says, "My name's Jesse, not bartender. Got that?"

"Sure," Jack responds.

Jesse opens our bottles and sticks out his hand for his money.

I look at the people having a good time here. My own grandfather could be here drinking beer, too. I realize that they all must be dead in my time. Now, though, they celebrate like young people in this young world. Time is so short, but they do not see that their time is ticking. Sooner or later time will come for them all in turn. One minute you're living and the next minute you're dead. This makes me think that we have so little time, so we should make every minute count.

"Here is your fifty cents, sir," Jack says.

Jack picks up his beer and says, "I drink this to 1914 and to you, my best friend who thought I was a little crazy. To you, Gunnar!"

"Thanks. I owe you for this." I raise my beer. "To you, Jack. I will always remember this day and the restaurant. I knew this man would be my friend someday, somehow. It turned out to be true. I'll always believe in you, Jack, despite your bad jokes."

I hear noise in the back of the saloon. Some men there are fighting about something. These men out here—they do know how to fight.

About five policemen are sitting and drinking beer, talking to one another. They do nothing about the fighting going on.

The bartender gets angry. He grabs a bat from behind the bar and says, "I'll be right back. I have to take care of this."

He goes over and hits one of the men on the head, sending him to the floor. He then looks at the other man standing there who sees the bat. He knows what's coming his way. He, too, is knocked down.

The police watch the whole thing but only drink their beer.

The bartender yells, "I'll give any two men a shot of whiskey for taking these bastards out of here! And you can take what money they have if you want it—I don't care—just get 'em out."

15

He looks around with bat in hand—ready for any other trouble that may arise in his bar.

He then returns to the bar and says, "That takes care of them."

Jack turns to me. "I think this beer is well worth twenty-five cents a bottle, don't you?"

"Yes. In our time we would be paying up the nose. And to see and touch this world we're in—it's priceless. If my brother only knew I was in the past right now—he'd never believe me."

"You know," Jack remarks, "there's a big different between 1914 and 2010. There are no cell phones out here, for one thing."

"Except for the one in my pocket.

"Hey! Are those cancan dancers?"

"They look damn good, don't they?" Jack comments. "I can never get enough of pretty women."

Then it occurs to me—"You know, they must be dead in our time. I wonder what kind of lives they lived beyond their life in this bar..."

"We all get old at some point—even us and we're time travelers! But these women are young now. Since we can go back in time, they can live again and stay young for us forever. They don't know that we are from a different time. This isn't our time and our time isn't theirs. But at this moment, we are all together here in 1914. Today is today. It's not tomorrow or next week."

I raise an eyebrow.

"Gunnar, if I hit your hand with this bottle, it would hurt, right?"

"Yes..."

"Well, if I hit one of those pretty ladies over there on her hand, it would also hurt, right?"

"Right..."

"My point is, you both would feel the same pain because you are both in the same time. Everything's the same."

"I get it, but it's hard to get 2010 out of my mind."

"You will. For now, just watch and enjoy these beautiful women. My, my, my..."

16

"They do know how to move their bodies, don't they?" I say.

"They sure do."

"That one on the right looks a bit like a woman I used to know a long time ago—before she told me to get lost. I liked her very much. Some women are hard to get out of your head. It just didn't work out. I still think about her now and then. This one sure is pretty, though."

"I think so, too," Jack says. "Sorry to hear about your lady friend. Just remember this—women come and go. Like days on the calendar, there's always other day."

"She liked to cook for me," I continue. "But when she burned the food she would just break down and cry. That's women for you...

You know, Gunnar, there are no good girls in here. If you got the money you got the honey. In fact, if you like that girl that looks like your friend, she's on me..."

"No thanks, Jack. I'm okay for now.

"Which one do you like best?"

"If I could," Jack replies, "I'd take them all home."

I look at the bartender who wipes his nose with his shirt and asks, "How's everything going here?"

"Can we get two more beers?" I ask, "I'll pay for these."

"Put your money away. I'm buying the drinks today."

"No, it's only fifty cents."

In a low voice, Jack says to me, "You can't buy the drinks here. Your money is not from this time period. They'll think it's counterfeit and throw us out. Therefore, I'm buying the drinks today. Is that okay with you or shall we fight the bartender and his baseball bat?"

"Gotcha," I reply. "But when we get back, I'm buying the drinks from then on—all the beer you can drink."

"I hope you have lots of money! I do like to drink a lot of beer!"

The bartender wipes his face with a dirty, stained rag which has likely never been washed. He then takes his wet cigar out and barks, "I don't care who buys the damn drinks so long as somebody does!"

"Cool down," Jack says, "*I'll* pay for two more of the same beer."

Jesse puts his slimy cigar back into his mouth and gets our drinks.

Jack looks across the room for a table. "Let's go over there and sit without that bald-headed bartender listening to every word we say."

The bartender eventually follows us to our table. He opens up our bottles and asks for fifty cents. Jack pays and thanks the man.

Jack drinks a bit more and looks over to the pretty women. "I like it when they dress up all pretty like that in dresses, don't you?"

"I sure do."

"Do you ever undress a woman with your eyes, Gunnar?"

"No, I prefer to do it with my hands."

The women begin dancing again on stage. They're very good.

One starts singing a beautiful song. She's in a nice blue dress. The way she sings—I can feel the song inside me.

"I never heard this song before," I whisper.

"Yeah, it's a real oldie."

I drink some more beer and then ask Jack, "What are you planning on doing tomorrow?"

"You're asking what I'm doing tomorrow? You mean tomorrow in 1914 or tomorrow in 2010 which is many years to come?"

"You got me again, Jack."

A woman comes up behind us. She's very hot and she's wearing my favorite—a red dress. She looks at us with a big smile.

"Hi, Jack. It's nice to see you again."

"Hi, Candy. How are you doing these days?—My, my, my—you always look so good to me."

"I'm fine. Did you come here to have a good time with me?"

"Oh yes."

"Naughty little boy…"

She calls her friend over. She's very pretty, too, in her blue dress.

"Clara," Candy says, "Jack's been a good friend for a long time. He never gets older. He always looks the same—Why is that?"

"If you must know, I do not drink or play around with women. I only lie about it all the time."

The ladies giggle.

Candy says, "This is Clara. She lives with me upstairs."

"Hello," Jack says. "I'd like you both to meet my friend, Gunnar."

"Hi, Clara," I say to her. "You have a sweet name, Candy."

"Thank you, Gunnar. You're very sweet, too."

"Clara," Jacks says, "would you like to sit with us and get to know my friend, Gunnar? No telling if he'll be coming back here again."

"I don't mind sitting with two good-looking men," she responds.

I tell them, "Jack and I only drink beer that costs twenty-five cents a bottle. We don't drink ten cent beers. If it's not twenty-five cents, we don't drink it. Otherwise, people would look down at us."

Clara looks at Jack and asks, "Is that the truth?"

"Well, do you see any ten cent bottles of beer on our table?"

"No."

I see the way Jack and Candy are looking at each other.

"You want to go upstairs, Jack, and have a good time?" she asks.

"You know it."

"You like me to do that thing to you upstairs don't you, Jack?"

"I sure do. Let's go. Better upstairs than down here, I always say. You know I have a sweet tooth for you, Candy. That's why I'm back. Once you've had some Candy, you always want some more."

Jack leans over and whispers to me, "Here's a twenty dollar bill. Have some fun if you know what I mean."

"Thanks. I'll pay you back when we get home."

Jack gets up. "Don't do anything I would do. I'll be back in a bit. I have to go take of care of some business upstairs. You know how it is. Have some fun before you go back home, Gunnar.

"Clara, watch out for Gunnar. He's a wild animal—like me."

He looks up and down at Clara's body. I know what he's thinking about doing with her, too.

He goes up with Candy by his side and a big smile on his face.

I look to Clara and try a little conversation. "It's a nice day today, don't you think?"

"Yes, it is a nice day today."

"Would you like another drink, Clara?"

"Yes, I'd like one of those expensive ones you and Jack like."

"Great, I'll be right back."

"Thank you, dear."

As I approach the bar I find our bartender friend, Jesse, pulling his finger from his nose and wiping it on his pants. Thinking nothing of it, he asks, "Can I help you?"

"Yes. I'd like two more of your expensive bottles of beer."

"Okay," he says as he turns around and gets them. He then takes the moist cigar out from his mouth and states, "That'll be fifty cents."

I give him the twenty dollar bill and he returns my change.

After thanking him, I pick up the bottles and start walking back to my table where I see another man in my chair. His shirt is really dirty. Doesn't anybody wash their clothes out here in 1914? He has holes in his pants and his face is scarred with burns. He's a lot bigger than me. I think he could kill me without even thinking about it.

"Sir," I tell him, "you're in my chair. Will you kindly get up?"

"I don't see your name on it—how do I know it's yours, mister?"

"Maybe you don't know how to read. If you knew who I was, you wouldn't still be there. You'd probably be running out of here now."

The man stands up, slowly turns and glares at me like I'm a dead man. He points at me with his big hand that looks like it could easily kill me and asks, "Are you somebody important like the President of the United States?"

I say to his face, "Let me tell you this—I'm not too happy with you in my chair. You should watch it—you never know what I'll do. I get real mad sometimes with people and I can't stop myself."

"From what?"

"Well, sir, if you're gunna play with fire you're gunna get burned. You should know that, judging by your face. And if you play with me you'll probably get hurt here today—badly."

"You looking for trouble?" the man asks.

20

"No, but *you're* asking for trouble with me. I was jailed for killing a man like you. I love killing with my hands. It feels so good inside. To see all the blood coming out… I did not want to kill that man but he had to die. He just made me go crazy and before I knew it, he was dead and my hands were covered in his blood.

"My doctor says I am a sick person. I don't know if he's right but he gave me some medicine to take. I did not take my medicine today. It takes the fire out of you and makes you a bit sleepy.

"Seeing a man's blood—it makes me go wild. I can't stop myself. And to touch it—I rubbed his blood all over my hands and face. You think I'm sick," I say as I laugh, "but it's so nice and warm!"

The man grows confused and apprehensive.

"If I have to see the judge again," I tell him, "I don't think he'll be very happy with me.

"But for a few bucks, my doctor will say anything. He would say, 'If he'd just taken my medicine… he would not have killed that man.'

"So if you do not get up from that chair right now, one person will live and one person will die. If we fight, you better kill me because I will not stop until I kill you. Up to you. You gunna die for that chair today? You must like it a lot to give your life for it. I don't care if I live or die because I know I'm a bad person who should die.

"First, though, could you help me out and write something for the judge? Tell him what happened and why I had to kill you and how I said I did not want any trouble and put your name on it. Or you know what—to hell with that damn letter! It's the blood I love! I'd like to see it one more time before I die—in my hands, my face and all over me. Is that alright with you, sir?"

"No, that's not alright with me. I think you're crazy."

"Yes, but I like it that way."

"You can have your damn chair back if you want it—it's yours."

He walks over to the bar. He looks back at me and I know he must be thinking of what a sick person I am.

"Did you really kill someone, Gunnar?" Clara asks.

21

"No, I was just talking myself out of a fight."

"You're a good talker, too!"

We start to relax and drink our beers in peace. I look to the people drinking and talking to one other at the bar, as if what they are saying is so important. In my time they are all dead so it doesn't matter what they say to me—I'll still be young in 2010 and they won't.

"Do you live far away from here, Gunnar?" Clara asks.

"Yes. Very far from here. Many days away."

"I ask because I have never seen you in here before. I would have remembered you."

"You wouldn't believe how I got here if I told you."

"Gunnar, do you want to go upstairs and have some fun? I know what a man wants. Will you let me show you a good time?"

"Uh, I think I know what you're saying, Clara."

"I'm not going to lie to you, Gunnar. This is how I make a living. Jack and Candy are having fun upstairs right now. I'll do anything to make you happy. Do you want me?"

"I like you, Clara, very much but I have never had to pay for sex before and so I'll have to say 'no' to you.

"How much do you get for taking a man upstairs?"

"Five dollars.

"I don't really like being with all these different men. My husband was killed in this saloon. We had no children. I can't read or write. So Candy offered me work here. What else could I do? I still need to eat so I live with her. If my husband could see me now…"

"How about this—I give you ten dollars to *not* have sex with me. We can just sit and talk like people do about your town or even your husband if you want to—I don't care—as long as I can look into your eyes. I'll just listen." I slide the money over to her.

"Thank you, Gunnar. I could use the money."

She puts the ten dollars in her pocket. "I never met a man like you here before. You got money but you don't want me for that. A woman doesn't see that often nowadays. Day or night, the men are only after one thing. Sometimes I think to myself, 'Can't a woman get any sleep around here?' They all talk a little but they'd rather get on with it and not talk at all. A woman knows these things. They don't think of me as a person but just a piece of meat. Except you. I like that."

We talk for a while longer until Jack and Candy eventually return from upstairs. Seeing us at the table, Jack says, "Clara, it's your turn! You ready to go upstairs and have some fun?"

I think he's had a bit too much to drink at this point.

He's looking over Clara's body like a wild animal in Africa, ready for the kill. "I've got five dollars in my hand and I want to get you upstairs in your bed. I'll take your clothes off one piece at a time until they're all on the floor and then the fun begins for you."

This is getting awkward.

Candy sees the way Jack is looking at her best friend. She knows what kind of man Jack is and what he will do with Clara upstairs. She obviously doesn't like it but doesn't say a word. I guess that's the way it is in a saloon in 1914 where the man is boss.

Clara says, "Gunnar almost got into a fight with that man there."

Jack looks to me and asks, "What happened?"

"I went to get some more beer and when I got back, he was sitting in my chair. We argued a little but eventually he let me have it back. But I'd rather not talk about it anymore if that's okay with you."

"Well," Jack says, "let's just drink some more beer then!"

I notice that everybody around us is just sitting there, staring at me without saying a word. Jack seems uncertain of what really happened so we just look at each other for a while.

Finally, Jack says, "I think it's about time to go. Ready, Gunnar?"

"Ah… Sure. Any time you are."

Jack looks to Clara and says, "I'll take you upstairs another time. But here's your five dollars anyway." He pats her on her behind.

"Well, Candy," I say, "it's been fun. Clara, maybe next time…"

No one says a word to Jack.

Clara asks me, "Will you be back someday? I like talking to you."

"If the possibility exists, I'll come back and see you again, Clara."

"Great. We'll have a lot of fun you wait and see. I promise you." She then whispers into my ear, "I'll show you what a woman can do for a man with love in her heart, something much greater than sex."

Jack gives Candy a big kiss and pats her bottom, too. "I'll see you again, Candy. Be good."

At the door, I turn and look at Clara—she has such beautiful eyes.

Walking up the street, Jack says, "Those women are a lot of fun. I'd sure like to get my hands on Clara. Women, though, come and go. That's the way it is for time travelers. Just have a good time. Women are like another day. Start a new day with a new woman. You'll find love is only a woman's word, not a man's."

"Not to me, Jack. It's a feeling for someone that you care for."

Jack smiles and says, "Okay, lover boy.

"See those empty bottles of whiskey over there and them boxes?"

"What about 'em?"

"Fill one of the boxes with those empty bottles for me."

"Why?"

"You'll find out."

We head back to where we parked with our box of empty bottles. As we approach, Jack presses twice on his ring and the time machine returns back into view.

Its doors open up as the craft rises about two feet off the ground. The wings slowly swing out from beneath, ready to fly once more. Its electric charge shimmers with that distinctive glow which envelops it. The colors of red, yellow and blue are so brilliant to the eye. You can just feel the power of this thing—enough to light a big city, I'm sure of it, with plenty left to spare.

As I look around this town, I think to myself that this will be the last time I will see it in 1914 or talk to Clara. I have to go back to my time and my home now where I belong.

"So long to all the pretty women in 1914," I say aloud.

The return of the time machine caused everyone to stop moving.

A man, all dressed up in a pretty suit and hat, was walking in front of a store. He has one foot on the ground and the other up in the air. I can't resist but to take his hat off and place it under of his raised foot.

Jack says to me, "Could you put those bottles in the trunk?"

Behind the time machine, I find a door which I open and place the box within it. I then come back around to the other side and sit in my soft bucket seat as the door begins to close.

Time starts to move once again.

The man outside steps onto his hat and pauses with a very puzzled expression. He puts a hand on his head and looks around but does not see us only a few yards away.

I turn to Jack and laugh as the man starts to curse.

Jack looks at the man and then looks at me. "Very funny, Gunnar. You're too much."

He then holds the steering wheel firmly as he pulls it back just a little at a time. The craft starts rising up to the sky. I can still see that electric glow coming from outside of it. The days start to go by very quickly. For every second, another day and another night passes us by as I look out the window.

After a few minutes of flight, Jack finds a good place to set down. He pushes the steering wheel and we descend as slow as a feather to the ground. The wings retract underneath and out of sight.

Looking out the window, I see only rocks. No people out here.

"What are we doing here?"

"I've taken us back to 1714. Nobody's made it out here yet."

Well that doesn't make me nervous…

We disembark and Jack tells me to take that box out of the trunk. He removes a few bottles and places them on some rocks and walks back to me. He pulls out two guns and holsters from a compartment in the trunk and hands one of each to me.

"Gunnar, go ahead and strap this on and put the gun in its holster."

This feels somewhat funny to me.

"See that bottle on the left?" he asks. "See if you can hit it."

25

I fire my weapon but miss. It's just too far away from me.

"Try again."

I miss the damn thing again. It's not as easy as you might think.

"Get a little closer this time. I know you'll hit it now."

Indeed, it is easier to hit at this range.

"Good shooting!" he shouts. "Just keep shooting at those bottles and get a feel for your gun."

I fire off a few more rounds.

"Excellent. Does it feel good to you?"

"It feels okay."

"Is your gun empty now?"

"Yes."

"Okay," Jack says, "now I want you to try to pull your gun out of your holster as fast as you can."

My first attempt is clumsy.

"Keep doing it until it feels natural. You're doing well."

I feel a bit awkward at first but I'm starting to get into it.

"Always remember that a gun can kill so take great care with it."

"I know that, Jack. I'm not as stupid as you think I am."

"Take it easy there! Don't get so mad with that gun in your hand!

"Now pull your gun out as quickly as you can and point it at that bottle over there on the end."

I try not to get so mad but I do feel like an idiot.

"Do it again and again," he instructs. "Your gun and holster must be very close to your hand at all times so you can pull it out quickly. You and your gun must be like one. You should feel the gun by your side at all times—the bullets within the gun as well—and know how many bullets are in it. Your life will depend on that. A gun should be like a woman to you. You always want it by your side—never too far. Never be frightened. When the time is right you will know what to do. Without thinking, your gun should be out and you only shoot to kill. Killing is no big deal. I've killed a lot of men in my time.

"Watch *me* this time and learn something," he says.

He goes for his gun like a flash. I don't even see his hand move and he hits the center of the bottle! Damn, he's good…

"That was some very good shooting there, Jack!"

Jack shows me how to reload my gun.

It's my turn again.

I clip one of the bottles!

"Not bad," he says. "You're getting better."

"How did you pull your gun so fast and still hit the bottle?"

"It can take years to learn how to do it that fast, but remember that your ass is on the line when it comes to a gunfight. First, look at the target you are shooting at. Stand as if you are going to pick it up. With your hand going toward the same direction as the bottle, raise your gun to it, instead, and shoot.

"The second thing is, don't be afraid of the person you are facing. It doesn't matter who he is or the words he might say to you. He will be dead in a second or two anyway. Your gun is always the answer. There is no reason you should be afraid of anyone large or small with that gun by your side. Just go for your gun and pull it out as fast as you can—your life will depend on it. Stop when you get to the rim of the holster. That's when you start to turn your gun, point and fire."

"Jack, why are we doing this?"

"Oh… we're going to Tombstone, Arizona in 1810—the town of Buffalo Bill! How about that? You gotta be good with a gun or you'll die out there all alone. You have to keep asking yourself if you want to live or die in that town. That's the law out there. You never know when you'll need to use your gun so you should be ready at all times."

"Okay, let's go."

"No, Gunnar. You're not ready—not yet—I can see that in you. Let's continue with the shooting until you are."

Hours of practice go by until it begins growing dark and my arm gets too tired to hold up the gun easily.

"Gunnar, do you feel ready to go to Tombstone, Arizona?"

"Let me just fire off my last shot. I know what to do now."

"Okay, show me what you got."

With my last round, I go for my gun as fast as I can and strike the bottle right in the center! My gun feels more like a part of me now.

I tell Jack, "I think I'll call her 'Betsy.'

Jack asks, "Now are you ready to go to Tombstone with me?"

"Let's go to 1810. No man had better get in my way if he knows what's good for him!"

We return to the time machine with our guns strapped on our legs.

I have lost my fear of this craft.

Jack holds onto the steering wheel with his right hand and pulls it back little by little as our glowing ship again takes to the sky.

Chapter 3: **Tombstone**

It appears like we're on fire as we streak along but I know it's just the power of the time machine working its magic.

Jack turns the steering wheel a little to the left and straight toward Tombstone, Arizona. He's very good with this flying ship of his.

"Gunnar, I want you to see something. We were in 1714 but now it's 2010 again. I think you will like this. See those buildings?"

"Yes."

"Okay, watch."

The time machine starts taking us back in time. It begins to make a funny "tick, tick, ticking" sound. One minute the buildings are there, the next minute they are gone, as if time had swallowed them up.

"Now they don't exist anymore because the time has changed."

The Sun is spinning around and around—coming and going over the horizon. Now different buildings stand in place of the other ones.

After a few minutes, we finally arrive at our destination of 1810.

Jack says, "Not too bad, heh?—to see time going by like that? It's quite beautiful, wouldn't you say?"

"Very impressive."

"I'm going to set us down over there by that store."

He pushes the steering wheel slightly. We come down slowly and land perfectly in front of the store, about ten yards from its stairs. Our doors open and the craft rises a bit off the ground so we can step out.

We climb out and I look around at this town that was here almost two-hundred years before my time. This isn't like on TV—this is real. I look at all of the motionless people who lived so long ago. They live once again for us as though we brought them back from the dead.

Jack leaves his door open so the people remain still.

He says, "First off, let's go in this store and buy a couple of shirts. We need to blend in with everyone else."

We enter and find its customers frozen in time. I find the need to step around some of them.

29

We look around for shirts that fit us. Some are too big or small.

Seeing a man standing by himself, I take some makeup from the counter and apply it to his face. I think I did a good job! His lipstick is even the right shade for his hair.

"Now he looks very pretty, doesn't he Jack?"

"No, I don't think so."

"Maybe he needs a pretty dress," I wonder aloud.

"Don't even think about doing that to this poor man!"

"Yes, but he could be real pretty!"

People here do look somewhat funny in their clothes. The women of our time would rather die than wear what these women have on. However, we are not in our time, we are in theirs.

I eventually see a dark brown shirt that I like.

"See how it looks on you first before we buy it," Jack instructs.

It does look quite good on me in the mirror.

"What do you think of this shirt, Gunnar?"

"Pine green. I think it looks good. What do you think of it?" I ask.

"It's okay," he replies. "These will only cost us ninety cents each. Prices aren't bad here in 1810. I'll leave them two dollars here on the cash box. The clerk will figure out what to do with it. Let's get out of this store before we become part of it."

Outside, Jack takes his old shirt off for his new one. He explains, "These shirts look too new to wear in this town so we'll make them look older by rubbing them in dirt. We'll blend in better that way."

I follow Jack's lead then shake off the excess dust and put it on.

I give Jack my old shirt and he stashes both in the time machine.

"Now we'll let these people come back to normal again," he says.

He closes his door and the craft lowers itself to the ground as its wings retract beneath it and vanishes altogether.

The town starts to move again.

"Now let's go and check out the past here for ourselves," he says. "Here we are in a town in 1810 in the Old West..."

I look through the store window. The women there notice the man with the makeup on his face and start to laugh.

The man looks puzzled and asks, "Why ya laughing at me?"

"Look in the mirror!" one woman says.

He does so and appears surprised at first, then grows very angry.

"Who did this?" he yells. "I'll kill the man who did this to me!"

He runs outside to get away from all the people laughing at him. He sees us there and runs away from us, too.

I look at Jack, he looks at me, and we both start to chuckle.

"Gunnar is my name and makeup is my game."

"You're too much. Think of what would have happened if you put that dress on him!"

Heading down the street I ask, "You smell something out here?"

"Yes I do—now that you mention it."

Looking around, we see manure all over the street.

He says, "Every horse in this town has to do their thing you know. They have carriages that take people to the post office or the store to buy food. Horses are like cars to them. From carriages come animals and animal waste. People just ride horses too.

"You know," I remark, "on TV the streets are always clean,"

"That's television for you. This, however, is Tombstone in 1810, not Hollywood in 2010. Can you see the stars of the show walking in manure? Or falling down in manure during a fight? What about a man kissing a woman while standing in and around manure?

"Anyway, let's get a drink. How about some whiskey this time?"

"Sounds like a plan to me," I say.

"Let's go to that saloon over there," Jack suggests.

"Whoa," I say. "I count at least five other saloons on this side of the street as well."

"Yes, they do like to drink in this town."

As we approach, we see two men arguing outside of the saloon.

One shouts to the other, "I know you slept with my woman when I was away and you knew she was my wife, too! For that, you will die

31

today! I hope it was worth it, dead man. Go for your gun and die like a man should die!"

The other man yells, "You couldn't pay me enough to sleep with your ugly wife—although every other man in this town has—even the blacksmith. She's like a used saddle—everyone's been on her. If I did not have to look at her ugly face, maybe then I'd screw her. But there are a lot of *good*-looking women around town. What makes you think I'd sleep with your ugly thing?" He positions himself to draw his gun. "If you go for your gun, *you're* gunna die, not me!"

Both men reach for their guns at the same time and fire. Both fall to the ground, dead.

I guess nobody will get her now. Maybe the blacksmith will.

"Don't worry, you'll get used to this," Jack says to me.

We move on into the saloon.

"It even has swinging doors like on TV," I say.

We enter like two cowboys in a movie and head right for the bar. Jack says, "Howdy, mister" to the bartender. "We'd like two bottles of your best whiskey. No glasses."

The bartender responds, "Two bottles of whiskey and no glasses. That's not too hard to remember."

This bartender's hair is a lot cleaner than that other guy's in 1914. His shirt is clean and white, too. He is a lot fatter, though. He looks like he eats very well here in 1810.

"Why bottles and no glasses?" I mumble to Jack.

"You think they care if glasses here are clean in 1810? And look at all the flies in this place."

"Good point."

"Let's go over there and sit down like people do in 1810," he says.

As we drink our whiskey in peace, I can hear some noise outside. I look through the window and see five men with guns dismounting their horses. They swing the doors wide open and approach the bar. One says to the bartender, "Blake, how about some beer over here?"

They're talking and laughing very loudly as if they own the place. One of them is quite dirty. He's a young man in a black hat, shirt and pants. He pushes his hat up and glares directly at us. I can tell he has something on his mind.

A moment later, he puts down his beer and looks over at us again. He then walks over to our table, puts his hand down, looks Jack in the face and says, "Mister, you're sitting at my table. I'll let it go this time but don't let it happen again. If you and your friend will kindly get up right now, there won't be any trouble here."

"Go away, cowboy," Jack says. "We'll have no trouble from you. Go sit your big ass at that table over there, big mouth."

The cowboy responds, "I don't want that table over there or any other table and I don't want any lip from you, mister. Get up now."

Jack responds, "I think when you were born you must have come out the wrong way—that's why you're an asshole.

"*Nobody* tells me where to sit and lives to talk about it—only my wife and my mother and you're neither. If you know what's good for you, you'll go because I'm getting real mad and that's not too good.

"But I'll tell you what—I'll give you my table if you first kiss my ass with my pants down. I think you'd like your lips on my ass."

"This is my table!" the cowboy yells. "You understand me? It will *always* will be mine until I say otherwise! Now get up!"

"Kiss my ass first."

The man's blood begins to boil.

Jack says, "You don't get who you're talking to, do you, asshole? Talking to me is like talking to death itself. You've never met a man like me before. I know that because if you did you'd be dead by now. Keep it up and you'll find out for yourself. Of course, it'll be too late for you by then. So go on back to the bar, boy, and drink some milk. Bartender, some of your best milk for this little boy here. It's on me."

Jack throws a dollar to the bartender.

The bartender says to the man, "Billy, come back over here with your friends before you get yourself in trouble."

"No!" he shouts. "I want my table! Get up, mister, and I mean it!"

Jack touches his hat, pushing it up a little to look at the cowboy a bit better. I can tell he's getting very angry. He looks up at Billy with cold eyes—eyes I have never seen in Jack before.

Jack says, "I don't like talking to children. Go tell your mother to come right now. I want to talk to her about her son and what a bad little boy he is. I think you will not make it to be a man. Today looks like it'll be your last day on Earth. The cemetery is full of people like you who got mad for something and get killed for nothing. You want to die for this damn table, boy? Does it mean that much to you?"

"I'm sick of you calling me a child," Billy says.

"You sure are acting like a child," Jack tells him. "You want me to clean your damn hears and noise, little boy?"

"Do you know who I am?" Billy asks.

Jack replies, "Yes, you are a jackass."

Billy turns to his friends, "Did you hear what he said about me?"

Jack adds, "Do not forget about 'little boy,' 'child' and 'asshole.' I just hope your mother comes and takes you home and puts you to bed before you get hurt."

The cowboy goes for his gun but Jack pulls his out first and fires two shots into him. Billy never even got his gun out of his holster.

On the floor, Billy moans in pain. "Somebody help me. Please—it hurts, I want my momma…"

Another cowboy goes over to him and drops to his knee. He looks into Billy's face and says, "He's dead. Billy is dead. You killed my friend here for that damn table! Was it really worth it?"

The cowboy stands with a very upset look and goes for his gun.

Without thinking about it, I quickly pull my gun from its holster, just as Jack taught me. I stop at the holster's rim, turn up and fire two shots into the cowboy. He falls backward onto the table and down to the floor with a very mean look on his face.

He reaches for his gun on the ground about a foot beyond him.

I fire a final shot and smoothly return my gun back to its holster.

Another man steps forward and says, "You're in big trouble here. Billy's father is in town. I know he's gunna kill both of you. He owns lots of land around here. He has a terrible temper, too. If I were you, I'd get out of town now before he finds out what you did to his son."

"Sounds like good advice, mister," Jack says. "Gunnar, let's go."

We only step a couple of feet when a fifty-year-old man walks on in wearing overalls, a cowboy hat and a large smile. Met with a quiet, tension-filled room, he sees Billy and his friend on the floor, dead. His face turns to dread as he runs to Billy. He looks into his lifeless face and slowly kneels to hold his son in his arms. He touches his hair and face. Tears fall from his eyes as he holds his son for the last time.

"Goodbye, my son," he says.

His head then snaps up to the crowd. "Who did this?" Somebody tell me who did this!"

One of the cowboys points his finger toward Jack and me. Billy's father nearly drops his dead son onto the floor and storms over to us. He looks at Jack in the face with eyes still red from crying and asks, "Did you kill my son—yes or no?"

Jack replies, "No, we did not kill your son… You did, old man."

"What are you talking about?" he asks in surprise.

"You are his father. A good father would not let his son in a place like this. If you were a good father, your son would be at home and not dead here on the floor. You let this happen to your son."

Outraged, Billy's father shouts, "I am going to kill you and your friend here before today is over with! You hear me? You will die here in this bar where you killed my son. You can count on it, mister!"

Jack interrupts with, "Get in line if you want to kill me, old man! It's not right to cut in line when it's not your turn. You'll have to wait about hundred years. You are not the first to want me dead and you won't be the last."

The man's face is turning red with rage.

"But today is your lucky day, sir," Jack says. "You can go on back home right now and be with your wife and your dog and cat and live a long time and be happy. Or, you can die right here and now next to your son on that floor you're standing on."

Jack quickly draws his gun, directs it at the man's face and says, "I will put a hole in your damn head the size of Texas—*and I mean it.* Your son did not listen to me and it cost him his life and it looks like you're next. I'm a serious man when it comes to guns and women and I do like women a whole lot more than you and your son. You want to live or do you want to die, old man? I mean business."

"I want to live. Don't kill me—please."

"You're talking about killing me and my best friend here, which I don't appreciate at all," Jack says.

"What's your name, old man?"

"Bob... Bob."

"Bob, I'm a little drunk today. Your life is in the hands of a drunk man right now and it does not look too good for you. You might die 'cause I had too much whiskey. Therefore, this is the whiskey talking. Nobody cares if a drunk man kills someone in this town."

Bob begins to shake.

"And by the way, Bob, this town here that you love so much—it smells like manure.

"Let me have one more drink before I say any more to you. This might greatly help you—or it might kill you. I don't care if I kill you or not. It's your life, not mine."

Jack drinks a gulp of whiskey and puts his bottle on the table.

He does look a bit drunk but that's Bob's problem now, not mine.

Jack finally says, "I've been drinking here for too long. So if I kill you it will be because of the whiskey I drank too much of. Therefore, I am sorry if I kill you today. I will just put on your Tombstone that 'This man was killed because Jack had too much whiskey.'

"You know, Bob," he continues, "I'm going to tell you something. You will not know what I'm talking about but I don't care—I will tell you anyway. You know... it's best to not drink and drive at the same time. It is the law. I thought you should know that. So the next time you drink and want to hop on your horse—don't do it.

"Is it okay that I call you 'Bob'?"

"Yes, it's okay. You're the one holding the gun here," he says.

"Bob, I want to kill you so badly right now for the way you are talking to me. But more correctly, it is really the whiskey that wants you dead, not me. You should know who is doing the talking.

"I like you, Bob...

"I didn't tell you this before, but I killed a man once named 'Bob.' I killed him 'cause he looked at me the wrong way. What could I do? He shouldn't have looked at me like that...

"Anyway, I know you're a bad father and I think you know it, too. However, I like you anyway. But your son had to die because of you."

Out of the corner of my eye, I see one of the cowboys going for his gun. On pure instinct, I go for my pistol as fast as I can. I fire one bullet into him and he falls to the ground, dead.

I go over and kick him and say, "He's dead. I didn't want to kill him but he gave me no choice. He won't be the last. It's in my blood to kill." I look down at his body and tell him, "You made me do this to you, you asshole! I'm sorry, but you did that to yourself.

"Who wants to die next?" I shout. "My gun wants to know and so do I! I still got a bullet in my gun—which one of you wants it?"

I walk back and say, "Sorry about that, Jack. He wanted to die so I helped him out there."

Jack turns and shouts, "Next time, if any of you men want to die, just say so. Gunnar here will be happy to help you out. We have the bullets and it's okay with my gun to kill any one of you."

A tall, thin cowboy with a white shirt and brown pants comes out from around the bar and glares at me with cold eyes. "I'm not scared of you, Gunnar. I have my own gun here and I know how to use it." He takes off his hat and sets it on the bar—never taking his eyes off me the whole time. "Now it's your turn to die. Are you ready to meet your maker down below?"

"You gunna put your life on the line to find out?" I ask.

"Yes, I am. Because *I'm* the fastest gun in this town."

I look at Jack and he looks at me. I look at this cowboy and say, "If you go for your gun, you'll find out that I'm a lot faster than you think. Your gun is just too heavy to pull out of its holster, just like the rest yours here in this town. But my gun is not so heavy. Where I live, they know how to make a gun. Up to you. My bullets are right here. Come and get 'em. They don't care if they kill you. I don't either.

"By the way, do you have a wife and children?"

"No, but I do have a pretty lady friend," he responds.

"Well, if you go for your gun and I kill you, I'll be sure to comfort her in my arms in her time of sorrow."

The cowboy goes for his gun. In a flash, I yank my own and fire. The bullet strikes him and spins him around. Not sure if I only grazed him—until he slumps to the floor.

"I told you."

But he's not dead. He whimpers, "Please don't touch my girl."

I reply, "I won't touch your woman now that you're dead, asshole. You didn't have to die, but you're still an asshole anyway."

Jack covers me as I load more bullets into my gun.

I see the bartender fumbling for a shotgun out of the corner of my eye. I turn and plant a bullet between his eyes. I did not want to kill him—he seemed like a good man—but he tried to intervene and this cost him his life. He slowly falls to the bar and then onto the floor.

All I can do is shake my head at how stupid these people are.

"Bob," Jack continues, "As I was saying, I hope I don't have to kill you today—oh look, there's a piece of dirt in your hair... Let me get that for you. Just don't get me mad or my gun may go off in your damn face." Jack slowly flicks the bit of dirt from Bob's hair with his loaded gun. "Just trying to do a good thing for you there...

"Now all of you take your guns off now and put 'em on the floor! I hope you know by now that we are serious people!"

After they do so, Jack shouts, "Now everyone get the hell out of here! Go outside and leave me and Gunnar alone. You hear me?"

They head out without their guns and without a word.

I see in Bob's face that he's quite angry. But since we have the guns, he remains silent. There's no telling what Jack would do to him if he did say something.

After a minute, I can hear them talking outside among themselves.

I then hear a man yelling, "This is Deputy Sheriff, Wyatt Earp!" He's wearing a brown jacket and black pants and a huge cowboy hat. "Drop your guns and come on out with your hands high up in the air!"

Peering out the window, I see about twenty armed men, looking very upset with us. Bob tells them, "Let's just go on in there and kill those two bastards right now and get it over with."

Wyatt Earp steps up and says, "No one else is gunna get hurt here today. You men understand me? I'm the law and you do what I say.

"You men in the saloon," he continues, "I want you to come out of there right now, without your guns. You hear? You won't be hurt. You have my word. You got five minutes or we're coming in!"

Bob says, "If we go in there, I want to be the one who kills them. You men hear what I say?"

I look at Jack. "Now what are we going to do?"

"No big deal, Gunnar. I've been in bigger trouble than this. We'll get out of this okay. You have *my* word on that."

"What are you thinking of doing?" I ask.

"First, we'll take all the bullets out of their guns. Then we'll have some fun."

"How are we supposed to do that?"

Jack holds up his hand. "See my ring?"

"Yes…"

"Watch." He presses once onto his ring. "Look out that window." Everything is frozen in time—even the horses!

He then tells me, "Look behind the bar and find a box."

"Here's a cigar box." I open it. There's a note inside it which says "I love you grandfather" and a picture of a house.

"Perfect," Jack says. "Let's go."

We go outside and start removing their ammunition and replacing their guns back into their hands.

"Let's go back in now," Jack says.

Jack goes behind the bar, gets a new bottle of whiskey and drinks. He then asks, "You ready?"

I nod.

He takes one more drink and then fiddles with his ring. Everyone out there starts moving again.

"You men coming out," Wyatt shouts, "or are we coming in there with guns firing to kill you?"

Jack shouts back, "Yes, we're coming out! Please don't shoot me or my friend here! He's a good person!

"Gunnar, keep your gun on at all times. Let's go have some fun with these hillbillies."

We walk out with our hands up in the air. Let the games begin!

About a dozen other men face us in the cold air. They look rather angry but I almost want to laugh for what they don't know.

"I told you men to come out without your guns on," Wyatt shouts. "Didn't you hear? It makes me look bad when you don't do as I say."

"Well," I explain, "if I leave my gun inside, someone could come along and take it. I might never see my gun again. That's the way it is in a small town like this."

"Tell you what—if you take your guns off right here and now, I'll see to it that they'll be okay. Is that alright with you two?"

"No, I don't think so," I reply. "This good friend of mine gave me this gun. It would break his little old heart and hurt his feelings if I just gave it away to you like that."

"If you don't take your damn guns off right now, I'll shoot you," the Sheriff barks. Your friend here will then see you die for that gun he gave you. Do you want that to happen instead?"

"Jack," I ask, "would it hurt your feelings if I gave your gun to Wyatt Earp here?"

"Yes it would, Gunnar, but it's up to you."

"What can I do?" I shout to Wyatt. "Jack's my best friend in the whole world so I'm afraid I must refuse."

Wyatt responds, "Be careful gentlemen. Just take your guns off now or I will blow you two away with this rifle."

Jack says, "Well, Gunnar—we've come to the end of the line. It's been nice knowing you. I'll miss you."

"Goodbye, Jack. It's been a lot of fun.

"But if I've learned one thing about this town—there's not one real man in it. I feel so sorry for the women in this town.

"Is it going to hurt when I die, Jack?"

"I don't know, Gunnar. I have never been dead before."

All the men look at us as if we're crazy.

Bob steps forward with his gun drawn, looks into Jack's eyes and says, "Wyatt, let me shoot this one. I want him to feel the bullet go in him. It would make me feel so much better."

Jack says, "Bob, do you really want to kill me after all we've been through together? I thought we were the best of friends. To find out we're not anymore hurts me more than you will ever know.

"If our roles were reversed, would it be alright to shoot you?"

"Yes! If you were the one holding the gun, it would!" Bob says.

"Well," Jack responds, "lucky for me you're not armed."

"We're the ones with our guns out! You two couldn't draw your guns fast enough to take all of us on."

"Go ahead and shoot me, then—if it will make you feel better."

Bob says, "I will shoot you first for killing my son and then I will shoot your best friend there for killing my son's friend."

"Go ahead. See if I care," Jack says. "I can take it. Because I am a man—a real man. Not like you or the others in this so-called town. You all act like a bunch of old women."

41

Bob points his gun at Jack's face and says, "Goodbye, Jack" and pulls the trigger.

"Bob!" the Sheriff shouts.

To Bob's surprise, nothing happens. He tries again and again with the same result. He then takes one of the other men's guns and tries it. Same thing. "I have to kill this man who has killed my son! All of you knew my Billy and you all knew he was a good boy who never looked for trouble or hurt anyone in his whole life. And this man here killed him for nothing and he must pay for it!"

Jack slowly lowers his hand and then lifts his gun from its holster. I follow. The men try shooting at us—but nothing happens.

Wyatt looks at me and Jack then aims his gun at the ground and pulls the trigger, with no result.

If you could only see their faces right now...

"Everyone throw your guns down!" I yell, as I fire at their feet.

Jack says, "Bob, remember what you said to me a minute ago? Let me see if I got this right—you said that if I had the gun, it would be okay for me to shoot you. Do you remember saying that to me? Well, I am the one with the gun now, Bob. Shall I shoot you now or later? Up to you. How do you want it—in your head perhaps?"

Bob replies, "I meant if our *roles* were reversed. I *do* want to live. Please don't kill me. Let me live!" He falls onto his knees. "I love my wife and she loves me. She'll have no one in this world and will have nothing. She needs me! You killed my only son. I must live for her!"

Jack says, "Your wife will not be alone for long because she will get a lot of money when you die. All the men in this town will want to marry her, then, so she'll be okay with her new husband.

"Two times I could have killed you but I let you live. Do I get any thanks for that? No. It does not pay to be good. You say I killed your 'good son.' I told you that you are responsible for killing him because you are a bad father."

"Yes, you did say that," Bob cries.

"Well, Bob, I don't know what I'm going to do with you. Should I kill you or let you live—it's a hard decision for me to make. I want to kill you so bad right now I can taste it."

Wyatt looks at Jack and Bob but there's nothing he can do.

"It is a good day to kill someone like you," Jack says. "Still, I'm sure there are a lot of other people who want to kill you more than I."

Jack strikes Bob in the face with his fist.

"How was that, Bob? Will that do it for you? I will let you live, you bastard.

"Now, everybody turn your backs to us right now," Jack shouts as he fires a shot at their feet. They quickly comply. "Nobody move an inch or you will feel a bullet inside you."

I tell him, "It's time to get out of this town."

Jack touches his ring two times, bringing everything to a stop.

The time machine appears, floating three feet above the ground, ready to take us back to where we belong in the year 2010. The doors slowly open. Its colorful electric energy lights up its skin. The wings are out, ready to fly. We step onto its folded-down doors.

But before getting in, I stop myself and look back at the cowboys. I say to them, "I'll see you in the movies."

I wonder if they'll talk about me as being the fastest gun in town. I could even be in a book…

We both take our seats and I close the door to the Wild West.

The people outside start moving again.

After a moment, all the cowboys turn and look back to where we were standing. I can faintly hear Bob telling the others in the distance, "Where'd they go? I have to kill that man! I will give any man here five-hundred dollars to find them for me! I promise you that I will kill them before I die!"

Jack shakes his head.

They all start frantically looking around for us. Bob has his gun on now and I can see him putting more bullets into it. I know he hopes to kill us today but he will have no such luck. We're just a few hundred feet away and they still can't find us. It's kind of funny that they can't see us but we can see them.

"You ready to go back home now?" Jack asks.

"Yes, I am."

Jack pulls on the steering wheel and we climb upward to the sky. I am so glad to be going back to our time. It's been a long day.

"You know, Jack, someone born here now would be dead of old age in our time. He could have lived to be a hundred years old, had a full life and had children. But for us, it's just a few minutes gone by."

"Yeah, that's the way it is as a time traveler. Other people get very old, very fast. But time always stays the same for us."

Chapter 4: **Gunnar's Future**

I can see the restaurant below where my time travelling adventure started and where it now ends. It feels good to see it in 2010.

Jack pushes the steering wheel down and brings the time machine down slowly by the old oak tree again.

"Jack, I thought you were a crazy man at one time, but I'll believe you the next time you tell me something like this again. It's been fun going through time with you. I will always remember this day. If you ever want to go back in time with me again, just give me a call."

Jack smiles and says, "Let's change out of these dirty shirts before we go into the restaurant. I'd like to talk to you some more. It would be good for us to leave our guns here, too, or people may talk..."

I chuckle as the doors open. The people around us freeze.

We get out and change our clothes.

I say to Jack, "I love this time machine of yours—more than any woman in this whole damn world!"

We take off our dirty shirts from 1810 and put on our clean ones. But when it comes to taking off my gun, I say to Jack, "It's hard to say 'Goodbye' to a gun that saved your life so many times."

"Yeah, I know what you mean. How about some coffee?"

"I'm buying the coffee this time," I tell him.

"Fine."

We close the doors and people start to move again.

Walking away from the time machine, it feels rather sad to say 'Goodbye' to it. After all, how many people can say they've traveled through time? No one but Jack and me.

By the time we cross the street, the time machine had lowered and vanished. I turn and look back to the old oak tree where it all started from, but it's gone—out there somewhere in time—no telling where.

We enter and see a booth over by the window. We sit and start to talk of our recent adventures as the waitress approaches our table.

"Are you ready to order?"

"Yes," I tell her. "I'll have two of your most expensive coffees for me and my best friend, Jack, please."

"Will that be it?"

"Yes, thank you."

I lean on over to Jack and remark, "That waitress is real pretty in her pink uniform…"

"She's not as pretty as Candy or Clara, though. I am right?"

"Women here are not as pretty as the ones in 1914," I reply.

I sit back in my chair and say with a satisfying grin on my face, "How time flies. One minute we're in 1914, the next minute we're in 1810 and now here we are in 2010. It's been a good day for us. I did stuff that no man could do without that machine of yours. Thanks so much for that. I will always remember being here with you."

The waitress arrives with our two cups of coffee and a big smile for me. I thank her and say to Jack, "She does have pretty eyes and a great smile on her. Something about a woman's eyes…"

"Yes, she does," Jack says, "Women are more important than time travel. You should know that. Time is time but women are women."

"You know," I say, "it was a lucky day for me when you came by here when you did. It was packed with so many people and you just walked on over to my table."

Jack smiles and says, "It wasn't luck at all, Gunnar. That's what I want to talk to you about."

Puzzled, I respond, "What do you mean?"

"Well, I actually saw you a couple of months ago. You just don't remember me. I recall it like it was yesterday. I overheard you saying to a man that you believe in time travel. I thought to myself, 'He's the one I've been looking for—someone like you!' Therefore, wherever you went—to work, to the mall or to the movies, I was there with you in my time machine. You just could not see or hear me."

"But why?"

"I wanted to know what kind of person you are."

"So you can take me back to 1810 with you?"

"Gunnar, I have been a time traveler for five years. I want to stop now and be like everybody else. I want you to take my place. That's all I ever wanted from you—to take over my job. It doesn't really pay anything but you'll be the boss. You decide where you want to go in time. And it's well worth more than money."

I'm speechless.

"I know you are the right man for the job. I knew that back in Tombstone. The way you talked to the cowboys in that saloon. When you talk, people listen because you're a serious person. And you're real good with a gun, too—a natural. And think of all the women!"

"Well, I did tell Clara that I'll be back to see her someday."

"Yes, you did say that to her…"

"You know you have the time bug in your blood now and it will not let you go. So it's yours, Gunnar, if you want it."

This really isn't much of a decision. "Yes, I'll do it. I do love that time machine of yours."

"No, Gunnar. It's not my time machine anymore—it's yours."

This is unbelievable.

"I'm done with my coffee now," I say. "How about you?"

"Sure am."

I leave a five-dollar bill on the table and we leave the restaurant.

We walk across the street to the old oak tree.

"Gunnar, here is my ring. It will save your life someday. Now the world is in your hands. What you do with it is up to you."

How about that—it's even the right size! It looks good on me, too. It makes me look even more handsome somehow.

"Just push once on that stone in the middle," Jack instructs, "and everything will freeze. Press twice and the time machine will appear."

I push the stone in the middle of my new ring two times and the time machine becomes visible and rises a few inches from the ground. Its wings unfold. Ah, and those gorgeous lights return…

"So everything stops when you open the doors or push the ring," Jack says. "Now get behind the wheel and get to know your craft."

47

We both climb in.

"Okay," he continues, "close the doors so people will move again. It's that switch over there. Remember that they still cannot see us.

"Next, I will teach you how to work the controls." Jack brings my attention to the dashboard. "This will display the year, month, day and hour when you push these buttons. For example, 1, 9, 1 and 4—that's 1914—and program these here to choose the month. Here is January or February or whatever you want. These are for days, hours, minutes and seconds. For am or pm, just push this..."

"Seems pretty straight-forward."

"Good. Now over here, this lets you speak in different languages. Do you know how to speak Greek, Gunnar?"

"Not really."

"No problem! Just push the numbers 7, 8, 23 and 4 and hit 'start.' It's all here in this manual. Just below the language is the number you type into the computer on the dashboard. You'll see this green light turn on and turn off and you can then speak and understand Greek!"

"That's pretty amazing!"

"Yeah! This manual has all the languages you will ever need. Just look up the language you want and the year."

"Does the time machine need water or anything?"

"It doesn't need a thing. But I will say this—whenever it acts up, the problem always gets fixed. One time, as a test, I put a mark under it and another on the ground so the two fit together. In the morning, they were moved about five inches apart. So the next time it acted up, I left a soda inside and the next day, it was gone! I think that someone does all of the repairing for me."

"Anyway, when you're finished with Greek, just push the same numbers as before—7, 8, 23 and 4. Then push this 'erase' button and the light will go on and off again. Your normal language will never be affected, in any case."

"I understand."

"In the dashboard is a box with more revealers. They let another person see the time machine. Give them one of these and it will also protect them from knives or guns. It creates a force field around them at all times. A bullet will stop an inch from their body and fall to the ground. They will always come back home safe and can't be killed in the future or the past."

"Wait. So we were never really in any harm back in Tombstone?"

Jack grins. "I could never find out how brave you really are when faced with danger if you knew you couldn't be hurt. And you learned something about yourself, didn't you?"

"I suppose I did."

"Anyway, on the floor is a pedal for how fast you want to go. To stop, just take your foot off. That's the only brake you have.

"Oh, in the back is another box. It contains five-hundred dollars in different kinds of money from different periods. Money for the 1950s, 1810, 1914 and some from the 1600s or 500 b.c.! There are also some gold coins. Gold is always good when you need money."

"Okay!" I say in delight.

"Here is my number if you need my help for anything. Give me a call anytime."

"Thanks, Jack, for everything you've done for me."

"No, I should thank you for being a time traveler for me, Gunnar. Take care of yourself. And be good to my baby here. She has always been good to me. She is in your hands now. You are the time traveler. Oh, and say 'hi' to Candy for me. I'm going to miss that body..."

"Jack, are you sure your want to give this up?"

"Gunnar, I met a beautiful woman who loves me. I love her, too, and want to be with her more than my time machine. It's time to stop. One day, it will happen to you, too. Some beautiful woman will come along and take you away from time travelling. Perhaps you and I will have another adventure or two. Nevertheless, this will be yours until you say otherwise. I cannot take it away from you now."

We step out and Jack closes the doors, returning time to its normal state for everyone as we talk for the last time together.

"Where are you planning on going first?" he asks.

"I would like to go… I think to 1956 and see the women out there. I read a book that said the women in that time know how to treat their men. I'll see for myself if it was the truth or not."

"Goodbye, Gunnar, and good luck out there."

"Farewell, Jack. It's been fun. You are my best friend forever."

"I knew this day was coming when I first met this woman. Words can't say what I feel for her… I better go before I start to cry."

I shake Jack's hand before he finally walks away by himself.

I open the doors to the time machine. Everybody stops moving, even Jack. I step in, close the doors and they all begin moving again. I hold the steering wheel for the first time without help. It's just me and my new time machine, now. I am a time traveler and this craft will go anywhere I want it to go—to the future or the past.

I program the dashboard for 1-9-5-6, then February, then 2. This will take me to February 2nd, 1956. I set it for a 9:00 am arrival.

"I'll be thinking of you, Jack," I say to myself as I pull back on the steering wheel and step on the pedal to go.

"Ready or not, here I come!"

Chapter 5: **A Rose in 1956**

A few minutes later and I'm in 1956.

I see a good place to park so I take her down slowly for the first time by myself. It seems to be working well so far. I push the steering wheel down, little by little until finally, I come down softly to a dead stop on the ground, just as I watched Jack do before.

I take a look around the town from inside. It looks okay from here. I don't see any wild animals or anything that would kill me.

"It's now or never," I say to myself.

I open my door. The people stop moving.

I get out and walk around to the back of my craft. I open the trunk and look for that box with all the money in it. There it is. I take some out and make sure it's from before 1956.

"I'll be back, my friend—my only friend out here in 1956," I say to my time machine, sitting there all alone.

I close my door and it goes from hovering, to a slow settle to the ground, wings retracting beneath. That distinctive energy glow fades away, with the rest of the time machine, from sight. With that, people start to move again as if nothing had happened.

I begin my walk down the street, passing a small park to my right.

There, I see some boys playing marbles on the ground. I ask them, "Who's wining?"

One enthusiastic little boy responds, "I am!"

I turn and walk further down the sidewalk.

I see other people going about their business.

I look around for the first time in a different time by myself and I wonder what new things will come my way. I have no idea. Without Jack, only time will tell me what will happen next.

I have no friends here that I can go to for help or talk to about this. I am all alone in that sense.

I stand on some grass and look around. I'm someplace in the past. I know that much so far.

No one noticed me coming out of the time machine, or knows how I got here from the future.

I can see things a lot differently, now in this familiar town for the first time. Things I never thought of before. Like the way people wear their clothes and the way they talk to one other. It's as if I were in a dream but awake somehow.

Walking further from my time machine, I see many cars driving by—some Chevrolet, some Oldsmobile, some are cars and others are trucks. They all seem so old to me, yet, are very new—especially to those people living here.

There's an old version of my Toyota pickup truck! I just love my Toyota truck.

I see a man fixing a flat tire. He doesn't look too happy right now.

More children are playing with their friends.

I see a little girl playing jacks as her mother watches. Another girl is playing jump rope on the sidewalk.

I look up and see a beautiful bird flying across the sky. I see more of them in the trees. I never really looked up to the sky much, before. I was always too busy to notice the trees, birds and flowers all around. But now I have time to really see this world of ours.

Up ahead is a sign. It says, "Restaurant. Good Food."

I could go for a good cup of coffee right now. I could also find out more about the people who live here.

Standing in front of the restaurant doors, I'm a little scared for the first time in my time travels. What's wrong with me? I've faced men with guns and bullets, and was not frightened by them. But now, I am very much afraid. I open the door and walk in slowly. I look around and decide to sit over by the counter, near the window.

There, a woman in a black dress and hat is reading a book while drinking coffee. I sit next to her and ask, "What are you reading?"

"Oh, it's a book about time travel by H. G. Wells. You read it?"

"Sure," I reply. "It's one of my favorites."

She asks, "Do you like time travel?"

"Excuse me?"

"Do you like time travel?"

"As a matter of fact, I am a time traveler, if you must know. I am from the year 2010. I even have my own time machine like the one in your book, there.

"What's your name?"

"Ramona."

"That's a nice name, Ramona.

"You do believe me, don't you—that I am a time traveler?"

She looks at me for a moment, inspecting my face and hair. It is a little long for this time period. She looks at my clothes and my shoes and asks, "Can I have a penny, sir?"

I go into my pocket, take out a penny and give it to her. She looks at it for a moment. Its date reads 2010. She then looks at me and says, "Yes—you are from the future!" She quickly shuts her book and asks, "Do you have something else from the future I can see?"

"Yes, I do. I have a telephone in my pocket. You can even use it."

I take out my cell phone and hand it to her. She looks at it for a moment and says, "It's a little small, but it is from the future…"

"Just push the buttons on the phone to enter a number," I instruct.

She enters her sister's number and holds it up to her ear. After a few seconds, she hears a response on the other end.

"Hi Leah. This is Ramona. I'm at the restaurant talking to you on this phone from the future that has no wire. I'm borrowing it from this man I met who is from the future, too."

I hear her sister asking, "You drinking again, Ramona? Don't lie."

"No! I'll talk to you about this later."

"Mom is looking for you. She says to come home right now."

"Okay, I'm on my way. Bye."

Ramona hands me back my phone and says, "Thank you. I do like your phone. You want to sell it?"

"No, it's not for sale but thanks anyway."

"Sir, I want to welcome you to 1956. I hope you like it here in my time. Here is your penny back."

"No, you keep it, Ramona. Something to remember me by."

"Thank you. I have to go now."

She walks over to the door, stops, looks back toward me and says, "H.G. Wells would be proud of you, sir." She then turns and leaves.

The waitress comes and says, "Ha! You almost had me going, too! You're a time traveler—funny!

"What can I get you?"

"I'd like a cup of coffee."

"Will that be all?"

"Yes.

"By the way," I inquire, "how much is a cup of coffee here?"

"Ten cents."

"Thanks."

In my time, it would cost about a dollar and ninety cents for a cup of coffee. Ten cents is a pretty good deal.

I look around and see only a few other people in here.

Today is the present for me. But it is also my past. So what comes tomorrow for these people, I have already seen yesterday. It's all just so strange. I can't believe this is really happening to me. Only if you could travel through time would know what I'm talking about.

As I sit with my cup of coffee, a pretty young lady walks in and looks around for a moment. All eyes are on her. She's like a shooting star that's come down to Earth from the sky. Everyone wants to see it, including me—except my eyes are on her beautiful body and face.

She walks toward me and it's like music in the air with each step she takes. She sits near me. I like that very much. Who wouldn't want a pretty woman to come and sit down by him?

She's wearing a white dress with a lovely pattern of flowers on it. It looks really good on her. In my time, you don't see many women wearing a dress like that. They like to wear pants like men. It's nice to see a woman wearing a dress now and then.

I ask her, "Nice day today, don't you think?"

"Yes, it is a nice day. Are you from around here?"

"No, I'm from another town called El Sobrante."

"What do you think of our town so far?"

"It looks like a nice place to live and raise a family.

"What do people do here for fun?"

"Well," she replies, "we do a lot of things—we go to the movies... Sometimes people just like to hold hands and go for walks in the park. I love dancing. To have someone you care for with you while moving to the music—especially if you love the same music—it's great."

"That sounds nice. I do like listening to good music now and then with someone I love in my arms. The time goes by so fast. But since I have no one right now, it's not really my thing.

"Don't get me wrong, I like dancing but not as much as I used to."

"I see," she responds.

"I know women like to dance a lot more than men do." I remark.

"That's true," she says, "for the most part men don't like to dance. You never see two men dancing together, do you?"

"You're definitely right about that. Men are just not into dancing as much for some reason."

She says, "I don't know why that is. If the music is good, why not dance your heart away? But I guess sometimes they do."

With a smile, I tell her, "When I have a few beers in me, I like to dance. My feet feel that music playing and I'm dancing on cloud nine. The floor feels so good to me then. If I'm dancing with a woman in my arms, I'll dance with her all night long as long as the music lasts."

As I talk, I look out the window and see children playing baseball. Sometimes, I wish I could be a kid again. In my time, those children are all grown-up, working and paying bills. They're no longer young. Time has moved on for them and for me too.

She then realizes something. "Oh! I have to telephone my mother. But I'll be right back." She heads for the phone booth near the door.

I want to offer my phone to her but that would just raise too many questions right now. She's a lot different person than Ramona.

I decide I will not talk to her about being from the future. Not yet. I will not speak of things to come such as wireless telephones, DVD players or microwave ovens.

The waitress comes over and asks if I would like more coffee.

"Yes. You make a good pot of coffee here."

She pours and says, "You're right, you know. Men don't like to dance like women do. A man would rather sit there all night drinking his beer without ever thinking that his girl wants to do something else. She'll just sit there watching the time go by as the music plays when her feet want to go out there and dance. I ask you, is that right?"

"No," I reply, "but what can you do? That's life I guess."

"What's your name?"

"My name is Mary."

"That's a real nice name."

"Why do you think so?"

"First of all, Jesus' mother was named Mary. Do you think Jesus' mother had a bad name?"

"No," she answers, "she did have a beautiful name. I like it."

A few minutes have gone by and my new lady friend returns from calling her mother. She sits in a chair closer to me this time. I like this very much. What a great first day in 1956! If Jack could see me now!

"So how's your mother," I ask.

"My mother's fine. She always wants to know where I am, like I was still a little girl. That's mothers for you."

It then occurs to me to say, "We've been talking this whole time, but I don't know your name. My name is Gunnar Best."

Mary interrupts with, "That's a pretty name, too."

I smile at her. No one has ever said my name was pretty before.

The young lady next to me responds, "I'm Rose. That's the same name my mother has."

56

"I like that name," I tell her. "It brings to mind a bouquet of roses. Everybody likes roses. Roses are red, pink, yellow and white—all are so beautiful, just like you."

"I never thought of my name like that before," she says. I like the way you put words together. You don't talk like other men in town. It's as if you're from another time."

"That's the truth! I'm from the future!"

They both start to laugh, even though it's the truth.

She asks me, "So you're not seeing anyone right now?"

"No, but I'm always looking. You never know where she will be. I do go out occasionally. When I see a pretty lady, I go over and talk. I may even get lucky and get her phone number and maybe a date will come out of it."

"You know," she says, "when a woman sees a man she may like, she will not go over to him. Why is that?"

Mary steps in with, "It's just not done these days. You don't know what kind of person he is."

I respond, "But you're talking to me now, are you not?"

"Yes, but you're different," Mary says. "You have something that makes me feel safe. I feel comfortable talking with you."

"Well," I say, "this is the first time I have ever been in this place before or spoken with you two ladies and I like talking to you, too."

Mary adds, "It's just not right talking to a man you don't know. You don't know a thing about him—who he is, where he comes from and what's on his mind."

"How long will you be in town?" Rose asks.

"I don't know. Only time will tell."

Some teenagers enter the restaurant and go over to the jukebox. They start up some music and begin dancing.

"To be young again one more time," I say. "It would be fun."

"Would you like to dance?" Rose asks.

"You know, there was a time when I loved dancing. But one day, I broke up with my girlfriend. She went her way and I went my way

57

and the music just stopped. There was just sadness in the air. For me, love was gone from the face of world. But I'm okay now to dance my heart away with you and start a new day and a new song.

"However, this music is just too fast for me right now. I'll dance with you if it's a slow one."

Eventually, a slow song begins to play.

"Let's go for it, Rose."

It feels so good to have her in my arms. Her small waist feels very good to the touch. Her perfume smells so sweet. Her hair is touching my face and it is so soft. I could go wild for her! I better hold myself back—who knows what could happen!

But then the music stops. It was a good song and a good dance.

"Gunnar, you are a good dancer. We have to do it again."

We dance for over an hour and it feels so great...

"How time flies when you're with a pretty woman."

"Speaking of time," Rose says, "I wish this day could last forever but I have to be going home now. I am so happy you came by to the restaurant today. I'll always remember this day in my heart."

"Rose, let me buy your cup of coffee. I can afford the ten cents."

"Thank you, Gunnar. I owe you a cup of coffee, then. Next time I see you, it will be on me."

"You got it, Rose. I'll come back one day and we can talk again."

Rose starts to leave but then returns and says, "Here is my phone number. See, you got lucky today! You give me a call if you want to. Maybe we can go out. How about that Gunnar, me asking a man out! You never heard that before have you?"

"Rose, I will call. You can count on that."

"Goodbye."

She then walks out in this world of 1956, in her white dress with flowers on it, as the wind moves it a little and her hair. She stops at the door and turns to look at me one last time with a smile on her face that could break a diamond in two. And then she is gone.

What a beautiful person. You don't see people like that in 2010.

I turn back around to finish my coffee.

A man walks in and sits at the counter.

His hair is golden yellow with a bit of red in the middle. He has makeup on his face and his lips are red.

"Can I have a glass of water, Mary?" he asks.

"Yes, Julio."

Mary brings it to him.

While my thoughts are still immersed in Rose, Mary says to me, "Gunnar, this is Julio."

"Nice to know you," I tell him.

He responds, "Your job is to know my name, do you hear me?"

He then gulps down his water, turns to me and asks, "What is my name, Gunnar?"

"Julio?—right?"

"Yes you are and don't forget it, Gunnar."

A young man walks into the restaurant.

Julio says, "He's nice looking…"

After staring for a moment, Julio gets up and walks out.

His pants are a little tight on him.

Now *that's* someone you would see in 2010.

"Mary," I say, "it's been fun but I have to go. But I will be back. You make a good cup of coffee here so you can count on that."

She looks at me with her pretty eyes and hands me a slip of paper. It has her phone number on it. I grin and put it in my pocket.

She looks like she wants to say something but can't find words.

I leave a dollar bill on the counter. "Goodbye, Mary. You do have a pretty name."

Walking out, I tell myself that it's been a good day so far in 1956.

Up the street, a sign reads "Esther's Flowers and Things." I think I'll go in there and see some of their pretty flowers. I have all the time in the world, with more to spare.

I begin looking around and smelling the different flowers.

A woman walks up and asks, "Can I help you, sir?"

59

"I was just looking around, but I thank you. Your flowers are very beautiful and they smell very good, too.

"How long have you worked here?" I ask.

"About three years. I actually own this shop."

"You do?" I respond. "You look too young to own a flower shop."

"Well, I should say the bank and I own this flower shop together."

"Oh, I see. So you must be Esther."

"That's right. Esther Segura."

"You know," I tell her, "only flowers can touch a woman's heart."

"It sounds like you know a lot about flowers and women, sir."

"I know a lot about flowers, but not women. Nobody knows about women. Not even women do.

"Where are you from?" I ask.

"I am from Mexico."

"Esther is not a Mexican name, is it?"

"I don't think so. But my mother liked to read the Bible and in it is a book named *Esther*. She liked it so much, she gave it to me."

"My name is Gunnar. It's not in the Bible, but it should be."

A man walks in and starts looking around.

Esther says, "Excuse me please for a minute," and she walks away to her new customer. She asks "Can I help you, sir?" with a big smile.

I could go for that kind of woman in a minute! She goes on to say, "I have some more nice flowers here that you might like to give."

I better go. She's really pretty, though. I'm leaving my heart here in a flower store in 1956. Boy, I wish she were mine. I decide to just walk out before I get too involved.

I go out and push my ring two times. My time machine appears as everyone freezes. I step in and set the controls for this date on 1980 at 3:00 pm and jump instantly through time.

Chapter 6: **Gunnar's Past**

Arriving at this 1980 version of the same place, I get out.

My time machine settles to the ground and is gone.

I see a taxi cab down the street. I call out to him and he stops. I get in and close the door. It's not a time machine but it will do. The driver asks me where I want to go.

"I'm going to Cutting Street. Do you know it?

"Yes," he says.

"Can you drive me to the fire station there?"

"You got it."

Driving along, I observe some of the stores we are passing. I say, "This town looks a lot different from the last time I saw it."

"Oh yeah? When was that?"

"About twenty-four years," I say—even though it was yesterday.

"How time flies," he says. "But we're here now, sir."

"How much do I owe you?"

"Three dollars is all I need."

I give him a five-dollar bill.

"Thank you, sir!"

I see the old fire station that still stands in my time. I remember it from when I was a little boy. I loved that tall tower it has. Now I am a man standing before it again. I've seen a lot of firefighters jump off of that tower while training. One of them is cutting the grass and he says "Hi" as I pass. I return his greeting.

It feels strange to be walking down this street again after so long. I can remember many of these people from when I was small. Looking down the street a ways, I see a row of government-owned apartment buildings, one of which, we used to live in. I see an old friend of mine playing out front. His name is Tom. In my time, he is in the hospital dying of cancer and there's nothing I can do about it to help him.

After a pause, I continue down the sidewalk before stopping dead in my tracks. There I am—I can see myself outside our old apartment building playing on the grass. To see myself—right there—before my own eyes is very hard for me. Eventually, I walk over to him and say, "Hi, Gunnar. How are you doing today?"

He—or I—say back, "Hi. Fine."

Look! There's my brother, James. He was cute as a child. It would go to his head if he heard me say that. He says "Hello," also. There's my little sister, Yolanda. I say "Hi" to her, too, but she does not say a word. That's a first for her!

Goodness… Here comes my father, driving up in his car which he parks in front. He climbs out, walks over and greets me.

"Can I help you, sir?" he asks.

"You must be Ray Best," I say. Here is my father—and he looks so young again—right here before my eyes.

"Yes, that's my name. Who are you?"

"My name's Gunnar." But what I want to say to him is, "I'm your son from the future. I came to see you one more time because you die in my time. I did not have time to say 'Goodbye' to you before, dad, so I thought I'd say 'Goodbye' to you now. Instead, though, I just say, "I know a man—his name is Joe Wear. He said he knew you."

"Yes, I know him. He's a good friend of mine."

"Well, he told me to stop by and say 'Hi' to you if I was around. He told me all about Lidia your lovely Mexican wife and your kids—little Gunnar, James, Yolanda, Gilbert and Anita."

With a smile, my father invites me into the house.

It feels so odd to see my father again since he died ten years ago. But there he is, standing in front me, looking so young.

The old ice cream truck pulls up in front of the house. All the kids in the neighborhood run up to it. They eagerly hand him money and he hands the ice cream over to the children.

We walk into the house and my father says, "Have a seat."

My mother walks in. She says "Hello." She looks very young, too. "Lidia," my father says, "this is Gunnar. He's a friend of Joe Wear."

She says to my father, "he looks a lot like you, Ray!"

"Yes, he does look like me a little."

"Would you like some coffee, Gunnar?" my father asks.

"Yes I would. Thank you."

"Lidia, can you make us some coffee?"

"Oh, yes."

As my father and I sit in the living room, I turn and see "myself" staring back at me. So is my brother, James. Yolanda is sitting nearby, not saying a word. I don't see Gilbert or Anita.

My mother makes a good cup of coffee. She arrives with it.

"That smells really good," I tell her.

"Thank you," she responds.

My father says, "I don't drink too much coffee. Just a little bit."

"My father is the same way," I tell him. "He only drinks a little when it's cold out."

He then starts talking of his job at the sugar factory. "It's fine, but I'm not happy there. Still, my children have to eat so I work."

"What would you like to do for a living?" I inquire.

"I would like to drive a big truck. A lot of men make a good living driving a truck these days."

"I think you can make a good living doing that," I tell him. "Still, I can also see you driving a big tractor—moving lots of dirt with it."

"Yes," my father says, "I would like that—driving a tractor..."

I then ask my mother, "Do you like going to the movies?"

"Oh, I don't have the time for that right now."

I say, "My mother likes going out to eat, then to a movie. Maybe your son Gunnar will take you one day when he's big."

"Only time will tell," she says. "It would be nice once in a while."

My father then asks me, "Would you like to eat with us?"

"I would like that very much."

My mother was making tortillas when I arrived. She goes back to finish them. When all the food is ready, we go and sit at the table.

My mother is a really good cook. Unlike my father, she's Mexican and dishes up some very good Mexican food—meat, beans, fried rice and a big stack of tortillas—real hot. It was so good to eat her cooking again. In my time she doesn't really cook.

I say to her, "My mother doesn't make tortillas anymore. She just buys them at the store. She says she's too old for that now."

"It can be a lot of work…" she responds.

"My brother doesn't like tortillas. He likes to eat bread instead."

She replies, "My son, James, is the same way."

My father says, "The first time I saw Lidia, I knew she was going to become my wife. I was working in a store and she came in one day. I followed her home and met her father that same day. I asked him, 'Could I marry your daughter, sir?' Shockingly, he looked deep in my eyes and said, 'Yes, but you be good to her or I will see you about it.' She then came to be my wife and we've been happy ever since."

I see in her eyes how happy she is and I know my father made the right choice. If nothing else, I would not have been born, otherwise.

Shortly after dinner I tell them I have to be going. "Goodbye, Ray. It was good getting to know you and your family, " I say as I shake his hand. "Goodbye, Lidia. You are a very good cook."

"Gracias. Bye, Gunnar."

I tell James, "Take care of your little brother, Gunnar."

As I go out the door, I say "Hello" to my other brother and sister, Gilbert and Anita, who are just walking in.

My father says, "Come back and see us again someday."

"I will see you all again in the future. You can count on it."

It then strikes me that I am older now than my father is.

As I walk out, I look back at them all for the last time in 1980.

Time must keep on ticking. I shall never return again. That would be wrong somehow. The past is gone. My mother and father are dead in my time. But for me, they will never die and will always live in my heart and mind until I die. "Goodbye, Mom and Dad," I say softly. "You were good parents but I have to go now."

I hear the door close behind me as I walk away from my family.

"God, take care of them for me."

I look around at my old home one more time.

I press my ring two times and everything around me stops and my time machine appears like always.

I open up the door and climb into the cockpit.

I look out the window and think, *If I could go anywhere in this world, at any time in history, where should I go? This world is a big place and it's all in my hands.*

I know. I'll go back home and see my brother, James, and tell him about all that has happened to me.

I set the computer for February 2, 2010. I think I'll arrive at about 3:00 pm. My lucky brother should be home then from looking at all of those pretty women at work.

I pull back on the steering wheel, step on the pedal a little and the time machine rises up to the sky. We're off for home...

Chapter 7: **Gunnar's Present**

Invisible to everyone else, I soon see home from high in the air.

I push down on the steering wheel and slowly my time machine comes down to the ground. I then let up a little more on the pedal.

I open my door, get out and close it behind me.

I walk into my house as the time machine settles to the ground and vanishes somewhere in time, waiting for me to call it back again.

My brother is watching TV.

"Can we talk for a bit, James?"

"What about?"

"Well, I met this man down at the restaurant. His name is Jack and he's a time traveler! He had a time machine that could go into the past or future. Whatever he wants to do, he can just do it!

"I went back with him to 1914 and then to 1810.

"When we got back, he gave his time machine to me!

"After that, I went to 1956 by myself and had some coffee with a very nice young woman…"

"Then, I went to 1980 to see Dad and Mother and we ate dinner! Oh, and I saw you there, too!—and Yolanda and Gilbert and Anita.

"Dad was so young again. Mother, too. You all were! I could not believe my eyes! If you were there, you would've felt the same way.

"Anyway, I came home to sleep for a bit and tell you about it."

James looks at me with a skeptical face.

"It's the truth! I know you don't believe me. I didn't believe Jack either until I actually saw and touched the past for myself."

"Well," James asks, "Where is this so-called time machine, then?"

"It's on the backyard lawn."

He gets up and goes to the window. "I don't see anything."

"It's invisible to you and everyone else, but it is out there all right, like a good old dog, believe me."

"Do you mind letting me see it?" he asks. "Is that okay with you? I was not born yesterday and I am your brother, you know."

"Okay, let's go outside and you'll see it with your own two eyes."

Standing out in front of the lawn, I say, "Here, brother. Hold this in your hand. Don't let go of it. It will let you see my time machine."

I press twice on my ring and everything stops as the time machine appears before us. My brother's eyes open wide as he sees it appear from nowhere. It starts to rise up a little and its doors begin to open. That glorious electric glow again washes over it and the wings extend proudly from beneath. It's ready to fly into time one more time.

"Oh my god! It's true!" James shouts. "I don't believe my eyes!"

"I told you, brother. Now you see for yourself. I was also telling you the truth about seeing Mother and Dad in 1980."

He approaches the passenger side and peeks into the open door. "What I can see looks amazing..."

"Get in for a better look."

He walks onto the door and climbs inside.

I get in from the other side.

"What do you think?"

"I don't know what to say about all this, Gunnar."

"Want to go for a ride?"

"Yeah!"

"Where do you want to go? To the past or to the future?" I ask.

He thinks about it.

"I know." I say, "Let's go to San Francisco. First, we can go and see the city by the Bay as it is now and then we'll go back and see it in the past. How about that?"

"Let's go for it."

I pull the steering wheel back and press down on the pedal as the time machine takes to the sky.

I can see its wings out the window over the city of San Francisco.

I program the computer and say, "Now watch this..."

James looks out the window and sees everything going in reverse. The days and nights go by so quickly—one after the other.

It's 1975 but time keeps moving back as I hold down the button.

"Pretty amazing, huh?"

"I still don't believe my own two eyes."

One moment, there's a building, the next, it's gone.

We reach 1940.

"Let's stop here," I tell James. "I'll put us down by that building."

I push the steering wheel down and give a little on the pedal. The time machine comes to a dead stop on the sidewalk right next to the building. Peering out the window, I see people walking all around us. Some walk right through us as we sit there.

"Pretty great, yes?"

"It's amazing!" James shouts.

"Look out that window, James. We are seeing the past right now. This world is in our hands. Today is May 5th, 1940. That is sixty-nine years that has gone by us. Let's get out and walk around this city of the past and get to know the people of this time."

"But they'll see us come out," he says.

"They can't see us if we're in here or if a door is open."

James opens his door, which flips down to the ground as the entire craft lifts up a little so we can step onto the door to get out.

As usual, the people stop moving.

"See—they can't see us. They can't even move."

My brother just sits there and stares at the people frozen in time.

"Get out of the damn machine, James! It's okay. Don't be afraid."

He finally gets out and I close the door as the vehicle vanishes.

The people start moving again as if nothing had happened.

"Come over here," I tell him. "See, it's gone now."

We walk down the streets of old San Francisco.

"This is a great city to visit," James says. "Let's go in here."

We enter a store and see what it holds.

"Do you see how much things cost here, Gunnar?"

"Yup. Things are cheap here in 1940."

A young woman asks us, "Can I help you find something, sirs?"

"We're just looking today but I thank you anyway," I tell her.

She says to my brother, "I like your shirt. Where did you buy it?"

I then jump in with, "A small store back East in New York."

"Oh, I've never seen a shirt like that before."

She then smiles and walks off.

My brother whispers, "I got this at All-mart in El Sobrante."

"I know that, James. However, that shirt and that All-mart won't be there until sixty years from now."

"Ah, yes," he responds.

We look around at all the "old stuff" for a bit then move on.

"Well," I say, "we've been walking around old San Francisco for a couple of hours now. Let's head back home."

"Okay, Gunnar. But one day, we'll have to do this again, okay?"

"Sure, if you want to."

As we walk back to where we parked, I push my ring two times and the time machine appears again.

My brother looks at all the frozen people. He sees a pretty woman, goes over, and gives her a big kiss on the lips.

"Okay," he says, "I'm ready to go now. I did my job. I made her day very happy with that."

The doors open and we enter the time machine.

It feels good to have my brother here with me in 1940.

The craft now begins to glow. It looks so thick with energy—like you could cut it with a knife.

The doors close and the people start to move again.

My brother looks at the woman he just kissed.

"She is so pretty to look at. Don't you think?" he asks.

"Yes, she's very pretty to look at."

"Her dress," he remarks, "is too long—just a foot off the ground."

"James, this is 1940 not 2010. That's how women dress."

"I think I love her, Gunnar. Did you see how she kissed me?"

"No, but I did see how you kissed her."

I pull the steering wheel back and stomp on the pedal and the time machine leaps up into the sky.

I enter the date of February 2, 2010—10:00 PM.

A few moments pass and I can now see our home down below us. I push on the steering wheel and let off a little on the pedal as we slowly descend to the ground.

We get out and enter our house.

Sitting in the living room, my brother says, "Going back in time—boy, that was just too much fun!"

"James, don't you tell anybody about my time machine."

"Why not?"

"A lot of people would like to get their hands on it and go back in time to change history, that's why. That could be very, very bad."

"Okay, brother. I won't tell a soul."

"Good. I think I'll go to my room now. I'm a bit tired."

"I think I'll do the same," he says. "Good night."

Lying in bed for a while, I eventually decide to write a letter.

It reads:

To whomever opens this letter,

My name is Gunnar Best. I am the one who now owns this time machine. My friend, Jack, said he left a drink in here one night when the craft was acting up and in the morning it was gone and the craft was fixed. He believes that someone is doing repairs on it as needed. Can we meet? Just say when and where and I'll be there.

Thanks,
Gunnar Best

I get up and put the note in the time machine.

In the morning, I check to see if there is any response.

There's a letter on the door. It says:

To: Gunnar Best. I will meet you on Feb 3, 2010 at 10:00 am at the restaurant where you met Jack.

Well, that's today!

I run back into the house and get dressed. I then go downstairs and climb into my time machine. I make my way to the restaurant where Jack and I drank coffee the first and last time. I set down close to the restaurant and look at the people walking around me.

I climb out and everybody immediately stops moving—except for one man. He walks toward me and says, "You must be Gunnar Best."

"Yes, I am."

"You may call me 'Jim,'" he says as he extends his hand to shake. "It's a pleasure to meet you, Earthman.

"So, you want to talk about this time machine you have here..."

"Yes, I do. I have many questions about it."

"Then follow me. We will travel to another world—to my world. It's not far outside your solar system. Everything you want to know about your time machine and time travel will be answered there."

"Go to another world, you said?"

"Yes. Did you not hear me?

"You will not perish. Your time machine will protect you after we leave the atmosphere. Simply follow me. I will stay just ahead of you. You will see my butt the whole way until we arrive at my world.

"We will need to travel very fast so really push the pedal to the ground. We need to go thousands of miles an hour to get to my world.

"Baby, here I come again," he softly says as he gets into his time machine and I get into mine.

I close my door and all the people start moving again.

His craft starts glowing with all kinds of color dancing on its skin. It starts to rise—very fast—so I really step on it, too.

I wonder what will happen. Will I die out there all alone? I guess I'll find out...

Chapter 8: **The Time Planet**

I say "Goodbye" to my world as I leave it behind.

Boy is Jim going fast! I'm flooring it just to keep up with him.

Sailing by the fiery Sun, my ship seems to be doing okay so far.

I think that's Mars over there…

I can see Saturn over there, too, as we leave our solar system.

Wow, I used to think that going ninety miles an hour was fast!

I hope I don't break down out here in outer space. If Jim doesn't notice, it's not like I can call anyone to help me way out here.

I'm now going many thousands of miles an hour. I still see Jim's glowing craft in front of me against the pitch blackness of space, but I can't see my own world anymore.

No humans from my world have seen what I'm seeing right now. Who would have thought five years ago that I'd be out here traveling through space! I'll also be the first person that I know of to go to another world with people who want to talk with me. I might be in a book someday, who knows!

Finally, I see a planet up ahead.

The other time machine enters its atmosphere. His craft glows red-hot as it flies through to the planet below. I steer my craft down. Soon it also gives off a red-hot glow. Through my windows I can see fire all around me but I seem to be okay—so far.

I ease off on the pedal and start settling down to the ground. I park next to Jim's time machine which has already landed.

Jim gets out and walks away without saying a damn word!

I get out and am a bit confused as to why he just left me like that, on this other world all by myself.

I see a man walking toward me. He is well dressed in a fine suit.

"Hello, Mr. Best," he says with a big smile as he extends his hand. "Welcome to planet *Antonion*. I am the Governor of this state. Please come with me for a short walk to my home. Your time machine will be okay here. You have my word."

"Thank you, sir."

After walking a little ways, I see a big house up ahead. It is large and round, similar to my house, which I thought was unique on Earth.

We arrive and walk inside.

"It is really pretty in here, Governor," I remark.

"Oh, thank you."

I'm seeing things I have never seen before—like the furniture and the flowers there on the table.

"Please sit here in my favorite chair, Mr. Best. It has been a long journey for you. I know because I have traveled to your Earth several times. You must be very thirsty. Would you like something to drink?"

"Yes, I would."

"You can call me 'John.' As I said before, I am Governor of this state. This is my home and this is my daughter, Karen."

"How do you do, Karen?"

She is wearing a white dress that looks very beautiful on her. She looks to be about eighteen years old.

"Thank you for having me in your home today," I say to them.

He asks Karen, "Can you get something for Mr. Best to drink?"

"I'll be right back," she responds.

"What do you think of our world so far, Mr. Best?"

"Please, call me 'Gunnar.'"

"I like that. It makes us friends from different worlds."

"Anyway, your planet looks quite remarkable to me."

A young girl walks into the room and greets me.

"This is my other daughter, Gail," John says. "She wanted to meet an Earthman."

Gail is wearing a light blue dress with something in her hair. She looks about ten years old.

"Hi, Gail. How are you doing?"

She replies, "Just fine, Earthman" as she laughs.

"John," I say, "you and your daughters speak really good English. Do you all speak my language here?"

"No, we don't speak a word of English. Our language is altogether different from yours but today we all get to speak it for you. We will go back to our own language tomorrow."

"But how is it that I can see and hear you speaking English now?"

"Do you remember the computer in your time machine that has all the different languages and numbers on it? There is also a book that goes with it which allows you to speak in any tongue?"

"Of course…"

"Well," he continues, "that same technology lets us communicate with you now. You are the first human being to come to our world. We are too far away for your spaceships to travel here. But now we will show you this world of ours. I think you will like it here."

Karen comes in with two glasses of something and serves it.

I drink some.

John asks, "What do you think of your drink?"

"I like it! What is it?"

"On Earth it would be like a beer with a bit of whiskey and lime. It has a little kick to it but it is a good drink."

"It sure is!

"John, I would like to know more about my time machine. How long has it been on my world?"

"Your time machine is the first to appear there. A man brought it over in 1910. He stayed for a while then gave it to someone else. That person then gave it to another and so on. It was around for thousands of years on our world prior to that."

"Why was it built?"

"It was first built to prevent wars—to stop people from fighting and killing each other. By going into the future, one can seek out wars and find how to stop them from happening. If it is a man who starts it, we talk to him. If that fails, we take his life before he gets into power. He does not know why we put him to death and we do not tell him. No war will then come to be. Everyone will live in peace and all those who were to die in that war will live and their children can be born.

"We have lived without war now for thousands of years because of our time machines and we are very happy about that. It is better to kill one man who wants war than to have thousands die for nothing. And for what? Remember Rome. They fought many bloody wars over land and the Roman Empire is now extinct. Yet, the land is still there. Did the Romans even own that land? Nobody really owns the land but many people have died for it."

"That seems logical," I say. "So can I go back in my Earth's time and stop the wars there before they start?"

"No, Gunnar. People who died a long time ago in your world—let them be. Let the dead be dead.

"Imagine this—you meet a beautiful girl in 2010 and you ask her to marry you. Your marriage is lovely and you are extremely happy. Then you find out she was not to be born but nearby is another lesser woman that you are to marry and have kids with instead."

"John, I have a friend I work with. He is a black man and he talks about how the white man brought his people to my country as slaves and were owned as property. He does not like the white man because of this. It happened two hundred years ago and they still talk about it as if it were yesterday. Can I go back and stop this from happening?"

"Yes, but the cost will be large. The history of your country and its people, black and white, will change because of you. You will take the lives of many black people who are now married with children in your country. There will then be fewer black people in your country. Their ancestors will have stayed in peace in Africa. Your friend will no longer live since he will never have been born."

"So things get pretty complicated."

"Yes, but if we can stop war on our planet, you can do the same. You can go anywhere in space and time and nobody can stop you. No bullet—nothing can harm you with what you have. We will not try to stop you either. Whatever you want to do is your choice.

"Let's just hope you make the right choices. You will be changing your country and your people. For good or bad, only time will tell."

"I'll have to think about it now," I say. "Some white men will be happy about all this and some will not. And I'm sure many black men would protest the idea that they will never be born.

"Before I do anything, I'll tell you what I decide."

"I will wait for your answer, good or bad."

"John, what do you do about people who break the laws here on your world?"

"Yes, we do have some people that break the law."

"Do you have prisons for them?"

"No, but we will arrest a person swiftly. We have two judges who listen to their case. If they are found guilty, they must pick another world to live on, away from the rest of us. We know that person will typically commit the same crime again sooner or later but it is not our problem if they do so elsewhere. They can choose any of twenty-one worlds. One is them is the planet Earth. They stay for one, five or ten years—whatever the judges say. It is a law that cannot be changed.

"We call the Earth, *Planet X.*

"You have murderers, sex offenders, addicts, criminals and every other sort of bad person there on your planet. Still, some end up liking it there and can stay if they so wish. We even give them the money to do so. The same goes for other planets. But after their time is up, they can still come home if they want to."

"Where do you get the money from Earth to give them?"

"We have people there who give them the money and any papers so they can live there. They know where to find the money. They may see a ship go down somewhere in time that was carrying a lot of gold. In their time machines, they can go in the water and retrieve it. When someone wants to stay, we will only give them ten thousand dollars. If they require more, they can go to your government. Your country pays millions of dollars to people who break the law. Not us, though. We will only pay ten thousand a person.

"Sometimes, when we take such a person to Earth, witnesses spot our crafts and report seeing a UFO, as they call it."

"I was in Tombstone, Arizona. A friend killed a young man there. I wonder, if he had lived, what kind of children would he have had?"

"Well, let me look that up for you..." He turns to his computer for a moment. "Yes, here it is. You were in Tombstone, Arizona in 1810. Yes, Jack killed a young man named 'Billy Johnson.' If he had lived, one of his decedents would have been Governor of California. But he was never born. He would've been one of the best Governors of that state, too. He would have helped a lot of homeless people, lowered taxes and would have been well liked.

"Eventually, he would have become the President of your country instead of John F. Kennedy, who would have lived.

"Can we go back and stop Jack from killing him?" I ask.

"No, Gunnar. Let the dead be dead. It's over with now. Let it be. Let John F. Kennedy be your President and meet his fate.

"Do you want to know about the men you killed in Tombstone— about their children and what they would have become?"

"No, John. But thank you anyway. Let the dead be dead."

John gets up and says, "Let's go now for a little walk so you can see more of our beautiful world."

Karen and Gail ask if they can go, too.

"Yes, you can come. Let's go," their father says.

Walking through downtown, people keep stopping to greet John, their Governor. He seems to be well liked. Some, however, seem to talk to him just to get to know me, the man from planet Earth.

"So, Gunnar, what you think about our world?"

"Well, I see many things I have never seen before. It seems like a wonderful place to live."

Many people are staring at me as we walk by.

There are some pretty women out here. They're out of this world! I would love to take one of them home with me to my planet.

One woman walks by and says "Hello" to John.

She is dressed in a very sexy black dress.

She asks, "What do we have here? Is this the one from Earth?"

She stands quite close to me—about two inches away from my face, taps my shoulder and asks, "Are you from that planet, Earth?"

"Yes, I am, if you must know."

"You are the first human I have seen on our planet.

"They say that Earthmen really know how to treat women in love on your world. Is that true, Gunnar?"

"How do you know my name?"

"People are talking about you. You're big news! It's not every day that someone from your world comes to our planet. You're the first."

"Well," I say, "to answer your question, yes, it's true. I make them happy and they make me happy."

"You see," she says, "even in this world they know about you.

"How long you are going to be here on this world of ours?"

"I don't know, actually."

She looks to John. "How long will this human being be here?"

John replies, "I do not know either. It is up to Gunnar, not me."

She turns to me and says, "I am Blanca. This is my body you are looking at. I know you want it because your eyes say so. If you want to know more about me, come to my home tonight and you will know a lot more about me. I can make you feel very happy if you want me to—like no woman you have ever had on Earth. I will show you my birthmark. You'll never guess where it is. Men are here for pleasure. Maybe I can help you out there."

Her body movies nicely as she walks away.

"John, who was that woman?"

"She lives close by. Would you like to see her again?"

"Who wouldn't?"

Walking down the street, I see a waterfall in the middle of town. It is big and has people on it carved out of stone. There are also carved birds flying over their heads but they do not move and have no wires holding them up in the air.

"How do the birds stay up in the air like that?"

"I do not know. But it is very pretty, don't you think?"

"Where I live," I explain, "people toss money into the water for good luck. I have not seen any money here."

"We do not have money on our world."

"How do you buy something without money?"

"I will show you."

We walk into one of the stores.

He picks up some candy and gives it to the woman at the counter. She puts it on a machine and it says how much it costs. John then puts his hand onto the machine. "That's it," he says. "This takes the money from my account. People here only pay by computer. Their money is available to them on all twenty-one worlds—except Earth. We only give money to the bad people who live there.

"We don't talk to your government or your people. All they know about us is the occasional 'UFO sighting.' Today is the first day we have spoken to someone from Planet X."

"I am honored," I tell him, "that you have picked me to speak with on behalf of Planet X."

"Remember," John says, "you're the one who asked to talk to us."

"That's true. But it's still an honor to be the first."

"Gunnar, remember this—whatever you do on our planet will be remembered for a long, long, time."

"Are you saying I shouldn't get drunk or misbehave and be good all the time?"

"Something like that."

"Well, in that case, can you please tell Blanca that I cannot see her tonight? I'm going to kick myself later for that..."

Karen and Gail chuckle and look at me with big smiles.

"Fine. Let's go back home," John says to his daughters and me.

While heading back I remark, "This is such a beautiful world you live in. You don't have any garbage out on the street."

"No, if someone is seen throwing garbage he will have to collect garbage for three months."

"I could live in a place like this—anyone would."

John says, "You can live here if you want. This can be your home away from home and you can see Blanca any time you want to."

"John, I am a poor man. I could not afford a place like this. Where I'm from, I hardly make any money at all."

"Gunnar, would you please follow me."

John leads me into a big building on top of another building.

"Here is an apartment," John says. "Let's go in and take a look."

It's a very pretty apartment. It's even furnished with nice things.

"Do you like it?" he asks.

"It's very nice, yes."

"It's yours, Gunnar. This is your new home away from home."

"What do you mean? A place like this would cost three-thousand dollars a month on my world—if you were lucky."

"Gunnar, you are the first to arrive here from Planet X. Consider this my way of saying, 'You are welcome here, Earthman.' All of this is free to you and once a month there will be five-thousand dollars in your account to buy whatever you want. But first, you must put your hand on this screen."

I do as John says.

"Gunnar, you now have five thousand dollars in your name. You can go to twenty worlds and buy whatever you want.

"This apartment will always be yours. In twenty years, it will still be your home. I am the Governor here and if I say so, it is law.

"Someone will come and clean it for you and air it out."

"Well, thanks! I think I'll stay the night then."

"Good. This over here plays music. If you want to listen to music from your world, simply push the button marked 'Planet X.' We have Television from your world, too. Just push 'Planet X' or 'E' here. The 'E' stands for Earth. To see the shows in English, push 'English.'

"If you need anything, give me a call. Here is my phone number. Just enter the numbers here and talk into it. I will answer your call and talk to you at any time day or night."

Karen says to me, "Let me show you to your sleeping room."

John goes on to say, "In this room are clothes for you. I hope you like them. You see, we know everything about you—even your size! Shoes are over here. Here is also something for to shave with in your shower room. You should have everything you need.

"Oh yes," he realizes, "in this next room is a way for you to speak in our language." He brings me there and explains, "Sit here and use these buttons as you would on your time machine. That light will go on and then off when complete. You can then read and write in our language, too. If you want to learn other languages, here is a book that tells you what numbers to input into the computer."

I say to them, "I want to thank you all very much for everything you have done for me today."

John smiles and says, "We have to be going now, Gunnar. I hope you like your new home here on our planet."

"Yes, it already feels like home for me, thank you."

John says to his daughters, "Girls, it's getting late…"

The girls walk to John and they hold hands. He takes something out from his pocket and presses it with his thumb and they vanish.

Boy, oh boy, what other amazing new things will I find out here? I'm sure not in Kansas anymore.

I sit for a while and look outside the window. It looks so pretty out there and I'm in here. I think I'll go out and get to know this town for myself and have a good time in this new world of theirs.

I take a shower first and shave.

I put my new clothes on. They look good on me.

This reminds me of Jack in Tombstone—when we dipped our new shirts in the dirt and wore them. Jack said to get it very dirty, so I did. I'll always remember that day. I dedicate this clean shirt to you, Jack, and to Tombstone, Arizona where we were cowboys for a day.

Looking in the mirror, the shoes look good on me, too.

You do look good, Gunnar. No question about it.

New world, here I come! Watch out woman! The tiger is here and I am hungry! I'm not stopping for nobody!

First, I'll learn to speak their language so I can talk to the women. I seat myself and push the buttons that John instructed. The light goes on and off. I step out of the room and say, "Hello, Jack." It's odd to hear myself talking a language that is not English. It feels different in my mouth somehow. I still think in English but it comes out changed.

On the table are some keys which I put in my pocket.

I go outside and walk down the street.

I see a nice place to eat so I go in.

I find a table, go over and sit down, and look around the place.

Other people around me are eating and some are drinking. It feels much like I am on my own world and not on some other.

The waiter approaches and asks, "What would you like, sir?"

I take a look at the menu. I do not know their food here at all.

I look up and see someone eating something that looks quite good so I say to the waiter, "I'll have what he's eating over there, please."

"I'll be back with your food shortly, sir," he responds.

"Thank you."

Another man comes to my table and asks, "What would you like to drink, sir?"

I look over and see a man drinking something that looks like beer. I tell him, "I'll have what he's having," as I point.

"I'll return with that soon, sir."

People are staring at me now.

The man returns with my drink. I taste it and it is very good. It has a little kick to it but I do like it.

People are still looking at me as if I did something wrong.

The waiter returns to my table with another man who asks, "Could you please pay for your food and drink now, sir?"

"Yes," I reply, "but why? Does everybody pay here first?"

"No, just you, sir. In fact, we ask that you just leave right now."

"Well, I have never been asked to leave a restaurant before in my life—at least not in a run-down place like this. I've been asked to get out of a few good places lots of times, though. I bet you don't even eat in this place, yourself. It's too run-down even for you. I am right?"

"You *dare* call my place run-down, sir?"

I reply, "What is so wrong with the food here that you have to pay first? Do you know of a *good* place where you have to do that? Only a run-down place would ask this of its customers."

He picks me up, drags me to the back and socks me.

I fall to the floor and go for my gun to kill this bastard but I do not have it with me. Damn it!

The waiter picks me up and restrains my hands behind me as the other man starts hitting me again and again in the face.

Blanca then walks into the restaurant and sees what is happening. She yells to them, "Oh, no! What are you doing to this man?"

"I'm kicking his ass! He has it coming for saying that my place is run-down."

She shouts, "Take your damn hands off of him right now!

"Robert," she continues, "do you know that you are a famous man today?" She looks at the waiter and says, "You both are."

Robert asks, "What are you talking about?"

"This is the very first human to visit our planet from Planet X and here you are kicking his ass. Everybody will be talking about you and your friend here for centuries to come. Wait until the Governor hears of this. What do you think he'll do? My, my—you are in big trouble, you know that? You are *dead men.*"

The two men look at each other with sudden apprehension.

"Why did you do this?" she asks.

The waiter explains, "Well, he looked at the menu like there was something wrong with it. He then looked around and asked for what someone else was eating. That did not seem right to me. Then he said he wanted to drink what another man was drinking. His behavior was insulting—so we asked him to pay first."

Robert interrupts. "He made fun of my restaurant so I hit him."

"Robert," she says, "if you went to a new planet and did not know their food, would you not also look at the other people to see what they were eating?"

"I just want him to pay and get the hell out of here!" Robert yells.

It occurs to me that John had given me his number. I call and hear him ask, "Gunnar? How are you doing tonight?"

"I've just been beaten up in a restaurant. Blanca is here with me."

"Let me speak to him," she says.

I hand her the phone.

"John, I'm at the base restaurant. You should come right away."

I can faintly hear Karen asking, "What happened?"

John replies, "Gunnar was beaten up in the base restaurant."

"I'll be there in a second," he tells Blanca.

"I'm going with you father..." Karen adds.

John and Karen arrive quickly.

"What happened here, Gunnar?" John inquires.

"It's a long story," I tell him.

Robert jumps in with, "I am so sorry for what I did, Governor!"

I tell Robert, "You're damn lucky we're not in Tombstone or you would be dead now. I'd take care of you two myself, with my gun."

"Blanca," the Governor says, "thanks for helping. I owe you one."

The police arrive and ask, "What happened here to this man?"

I explain, "I ordered food and drink and this man said he wanted me to pay first. I asked if everybody here pays first and he said 'No,' just I do. I did not think that was right. Before I knew it, he and this waiter were hitting me. Blanca came and stopped them."

Robert says to the police, "I'm so sorry! I did not know he is from another world. I can't imagine what he must think of us now. Please forgive me, sir," he says to me, "I'll never do this to anyone again!"

The police officer asks, "So that *is* what happened here?"

Robert replies, "Yes, it is."

"You'll be hearing back from us tonight," the officer says to him. "You better stay in town. Do you understand?"

"Of course," Robert replies.

The Governor says, "I have to take this man to the doctor now."

"Yes, Governor," the officer responds.

John and Karen hold my hand as he takes a small device out of his pocket and pushes it. A second later, we are in the doctor's office.

A nurse walks in and asks, "What happened?"

The Governor answers, "Gunnar, here, is from Planet X. He was beaten by two men this evening."

The nurse asks, "He is the one from Planet X? Please wait here, Governor, as I take him for a few moments."

We go into a little room and she takes off my shirt.

"Sit here," she says.

"I hear that men from your world know how to treat a woman. Is that true? And that they are good lovers, too?"

"I don't know what you're talking about."

"Yes you do. You have a nice body. Your muscles are so hard and feel so good to the touch."

"Um..." I start to say.

"Where does it hurt?" she asks as she starts touching me all over. "Does it hurt here or over here or down here?"

"Well, I..."

"How would you like to come to my home?" She asks. "I'd make you feel much better."

"I'm not sure..."

"I like you Mr. Human Being," she continues, "man from Planet X, X and X. But I would like you a lot better at my house, in my bed."

"I'm going home now," I tell her, "but thank you anyway."

"Here is my number if you change your mind. Call me and you'll see what a nurse here can do for you, Earthman. You'll feel very good when I am done but you will be a little tired."

"Thank you, nurse, but I'm going now."

I walk out of the room.

John asks, "So what's the matter, Gunnar?"

"I am okay, John. I'll live."

I think to myself, "What's wrong with the women on this planet?" It's like they haven't seen a man in a very long time. All she wanted was go to bed with me. There's nothing wrong with that but on Earth, women are so different. You say "Hello" and they act like you didn't say a damn thing. On this planet, you say "Hello" and they want to go to bed with you then and there. I could be the greatest lover this world has ever known. But I like to go after a woman myself. I don't like it when they come after me. It's not wrong, it's just not right for me.

Karen says to John, "Gunnar wants to go home. I'll take him."

"I'll be there in a bit," John says. "I want to talk to the doctor."

Karen holds my hand.

I look at the nurse's lips. They look so hot. On my world, I would go for that in a minute but I'm not on my world right now.

The nurse says, "I'll see you, Gunnar. I hope you feel better."

A second later and I'm back home as my front door opens in front of me. It's good to be home again, even if I am thousands of miles away from my real home on Earth.

Karen sits me down and asks, "How are you feeling now?"

"A little sore but okay."

"Why didn't you just stay in the hospital so they can help you?"

"Well, between you and me, that nurse wants to play love games. She wanted to touch me all over—and I do mean all over. And I don't mean like a nurse, but like a woman in lust who wants to touch a man in all the wrong places—if you know what I mean. I just wanted to go home. I felt like a piece of meat with her.

"What's wrong with the women on this world of yours?"

I hear John outside. I yell out, "Come on in, John. Door's open."

John enters with a doctor.

"Hello, Gunnar," the doctor says. "Had some bad luck tonight?"

"You could say that."

"You came a long way to our world. Let me see if you're okay."

87

As he does so, it occurs to me to ask, "Doctor, could I ask you a question about medicine?"

"Please do."

"I have a friend back home on Earth that has cancer and is dying. The doctors there say there is nothing they can do for him."

"That is an old word to me—cancer," he says. "I have not heard it in years. On your world it is a serious disease where some cells in the body grow faster than normal and destroy healthy organs and tissues."

"What do you mean by 'old word' doctor?"

"That's and old disease here on our world, Gunnar. We don't have it anymore. Nobody does."

"Can you help my friend who has it?"

"Why, yes, I can," he says with delight. "Here in my bag I have some pills. Just give him just one pill and the cancer will be gone."

"Why give me so many pills, then?"

"One day, you will meet someone else who has cancer and you'll wish that you had gotten some more pills from 'that doctor over there on that planet' when you were here. I just saved you a long trip."

"It is a long trip, yes. Thank you for myself and my friend."

"Any friend of yours from Planet X is a friend of mine. But do not tell anyone on Earth about these pills or that you got them from here. We do not speak to your people. That's the way it is and it's the law."

"You look fine to me. I must be getting back to the hospital now." "Take care. It's been nice meeting you, Earthman."

"Thanks again," I tell him.

He pulls out a small device from his pocket and is gone.

"John," I ask, "what kind of device was that in this hand?"

"On your world, you use cars to get around. But here, we use this technology instead."

"How does it work?"

"Let me show you. Use these keys to enter the destination. If you want to go to the store downtown, and its number is 3754, just type that in and push the green button and you're gone, just like that."

"It must have a lot of power to do that."

"No, satellites supply the power. See this copper area on the back? It senses your hand and sends signals out from your body to anywhere in the world. It is called a *conductor*. I have one for you."

He pokes his head out the front door and mumbles something to a man who then hands him a conductor.

"Here you go, Gunnar. I had it made for you before you came. Here is also a manual about how it works. It is in English for you."

"Thank you."

"I know you have satellites on your world," he says. "I think it'll work okay there, too."

"John, how do I get of a hold of Blanca tonight?"

"This conductor is also a phone that works with the satellites. Just enter Blanca's name and it will supply her number. To go to her, push the green button. To call her, push the orange button. That's it."

I enter her name and number. I hear her voice saying "Hello?"

"Blanca, this is Gunnar. How are you doing?"

"I am fine, Earthman. Why do you ask?"

"How would you like to go out tonight and have some fun?"

"I would love to go out with you anytime you want."

"I'll meet you in one hour in front of the restaurant. You know the one I mean. The one I got my ass kicked in."

"Okay, I'll see you there in one hour. Bye."

"Bye."

John asks, "Do you feel well enough to go out?"

"My body says 'No' but my heart says 'Yes.' I feel well enough to go out with a woman like that. I'm just going to take a hot shower. I'll be okay. Besides, I'll be with Blanca and you know she can take care of me. What could go wrong with her by my side?"

"Very well," John responds. "You can use the conductor to go to the restaurant. Just enter 5559 and it will take you there."

"Thanks."

89

"You hold on to that. It's yours now, Gunnar. If you need to call me just enter 48—that's my number."

"You got it, John. And I will be a good boy."

"Have a good time. Good night."

"Good night, Governor."

I take my shower and get dressed.

As I walk out of my house, I think about my gun. I cannot take it with me. If I had it when I was with those men, they'd be dead now. Sometimes a gun is not the answer, Jack.

I decide not to use the conductor to go to the restaurant. I want to see as much of this place as I can before I go back home to my world.

I see Blanca up ahead. She looks so good.

She asks, "What do you have in mind for our evening, Gunnar?"

"Let's go where we can have some fun—where there is dancing and drinking."

Blanca thinks. "I know the right place. I think you will like it."

We head down the street until we see a place that says "Saloon." It looks like the saloons on Earth from a long time ago. It looks good to me. It reminds me of my home on Earth.

We go in. I see a good table and take us over to it.

A waiter arrives and asks, "Can I help you?"

I say to Blanca, "You'd better order the drinks."

She says, "Two beers."

"I was not expecting that," I express. "I do like beer, especially if it's nice and cold."

After a short while, the waiter brings our drinks.

It sure looks like beer but sure doesn't taste like it. It's different somehow. It, too, has a little kick to it but it's not bad.

The waiter asks for ten dollars. I put my hand on the plate.

"Thank you, sir."

That's the first time I used my hand to pay for drinks. Kind of fun.

Many people are drinking this so-called beer they have here.

Blanca asks, "Does this place look like a saloon on your world?"

"It does look a lot like Earth from a long time ago. I was in a real saloon in Tombstone, Arizona and everyone had guns. I was with my friend, Jack, and he was real good with his gun. I also carried a gun by my side at all times. One cowboy came over and told us to get up. Jack refused. They argued for a bit and the cowboy went for his gun. Jack had no choice but to use his and before you could wink an eye, he fired two bullets into the cowboy and killed him."

"Were you frightened?"

"No, not with my gun by my side. Another cowboy went for his gun and I pulled mine out of its holster as fast as I could and fired two shots at him and he went down. I had to kill him. It's kill or be killed in that town. The gun is the law there so you have to be fast or die."

The man at the next table stops talking to his friend and leans over to me and says, "I heard what you said to that young woman—that you're fast with a gun."

"Pretty fast. Why?" I ask.

"In this place," he says, "*I* am the fastest gun. You want to show your girl there that you're faster than me?"

"You want to die?" I ask, "Besides, I don't have the need to show her anything. I know how fast I am and that I'm faster than you."

"*I am* the fastest gun that lives," he shouts.

"No," I respond, "there is always someone faster. Like my friend, Jack. He's a lot faster than you and me put together."

The man says, "I think you're just talk."

"Didn't you hear what I said about my gunfight in the Old West? Do you want to be another one of those dead bodies?"

He shouts loudly, "This man says he's faster than me with a gun! Who here thinks he is?"

Blanca responds, "I think he's a lot faster than you, big mouth."

I say to him, "So what—if I'm faster than you? It's no big deal."

"Are you faster than me, cowboy?" he asks. "Or is your girlfriend the only one that thinks so?"

"I don't have my gun with me. But if I did, you would be in big trouble right now. You might even be dead, mister."

"We have guns here," he says. "We don't use real bullets, though, since we don't want people like you getting killed."

I tell Blanca, "My friend, Jack, would not like this at all."

I turn to the man and say, "My friend said to me that you only use your gun to kill someone like you. But let's go for it, dead man."

The bartender places a gun and holster on the counter.

"Take it," my challenger says. "Let's see how fast you really are."

A lot of people are looking at us now.

Why am I in an Old West saloon on another planet with a gun on? What a strange situation I find myself in. But it does feel good.

I tell him, "If we were in the Old West and you called me out with your gun on, by the time you touched it you would already have two bullets in you. To you, this is a game. To me, this is life or death."

He responds, "We'll find out who'd be the dead man here, mister. Bartender—my gun now."

The bartender hands the man his gun and holster. He straps it on and says, "Let's do it."

I strap on my gun. I place it low, close to my hand.

"Okay, you stand over there," the bartender instructs, "and you go on over there." We walk to this area in the middle of the room.

I look at Blanca sitting there, so beautiful. She looks at me but her eyes are also on the other man with his gun.

My opponent says, "Wait until you see that light over there go on then pull your gun as fast as you can and fire."

I check my gun. It has blanks in it. This man will live.

"You two ready?" the bartender asks.

"Ready," we answer.

"I'm going to call you Billy," I tell the other man, "because Billy is dead and so would you be if we had real bullets in our guns."

The light goes on. I go for my gun and fire two shots.

The other man still has his gun in his holster.

"You're dead, Billy," I say to him. "Let's do it again, dead man."

He looks at me with an astonished face.

This time I cross my arms before the light goes on. I pull out my gun and fire two more shots and again, his gun is still in its holster.

"You're dead again, Billy."

The bartender says, "Chad, if that gun had real bullets you'd be dead right now."

"One more time, Chad?" I ask. "With real bullets this time?"

"No way!" Chad responds. "You're too fast for me."

Another man approaches me and asks, "What is your name, sir?"

"My name is Gunnar Best."

"You are the fastest man with a gun I have ever seen. You're the one from Planet X, yes?"

"That's right."

"So you're the one everyone's talking about. I heard that you were here on our planet but I did not know you were coming to my saloon! We don't get many famous people in here, sir."

He calls for the waitress. She is very nice to look at. Mamma Mia! He tells her, "All the drinks for this table are on the house."

I ask him, "What is your name, sir?"

"My name is Toby. I am the owner of this establishment."

"This is my friend, Blanca," I tell him. "She is from your planet."

"Please sit down and enjoy yourselves," he tells us. "What would you like to drink?"

"Two beers would be good for now," I respond.

"You got it! If there is anything else, just let me know.

"Is it okay for me to call you Gunnar, Earthman?"

"I don't mind at all, Toby."

"You are the first human being I have ever seen, you know that? You look just like one of us here on our planet, don't you?"

"So far as I can tell," I reply.

"We don't all look the same," Blanca says. "Look around us. Like any planet, we still have different races. Some may surprise you."

Toby adds, "On some planets in our solar system, people do not look like us. Some look rather ugly with big eyes and gray skin. They are bad people and I understand they go to your planet, take some of your people and do tests on them. Some are even killed. If I may give you some advice, if you see them you should definitely *attack them.* They will kill you if they can but you are safe here in my place."

The waitress brings our beers.

"I will leave you to your drinks," Toby says. "Enjoy yourselves."

"Thank you," Blanca and I reply.

Chad approaches our table and says, "I'm sorry if the way I spoke was wrong of me, Earthman."

"It okay." I then lean to Blanca and whisper something in her ear. I turn to Chad and ask, "Would you like to join us for a beer?"

He says, "Yes, I do like beer! Blanca, is that okay with you?"

She responds, "Yes, please join us, Chad."

Chad tells me, "You are the fastest with a gun I have ever seen."

"That may be, but my teacher, Jack, is much faster than I am. You can't even see his hand move when he goes for his gun."

Two young women come over to our table. One of them asks me, "Are you really from Planet X?"

"Yes, I am."

I cannot believe that I have two such pretty women talking to me right now. Oh my god, I am so lucky today. What a world!

I can see in Blanca's eyes that she is not too happy about all this.

The other woman asks, "Can we sit here with you, Earthman?"

Chad says, "Yes! You can even sit on my lap if you want to!"

They're dressed like cowgirls with cowboy hats. They have very nice bodies but I told John I would be good. It won't be easy.

One of the women asks, "How is it on your Planet X?"

"It's similar to here," I answer.

"I understand they do a lot of fighting on your world."

"Yes, but here on your planet, I was just buying some food and a drink and got my butt kicked about three hours ago."

"No way!" Chad says. "Not here on *this* planet!"

"Sure!" I tell him. "Just around the block at a restaurant. I got my butt kicked by this guy named Robert who owns the place. One of the waiters there held my arms behind me as I was beaten. Then Blanca came in and stopped them.

"Then, after all that," I say to Chad, "I came in here with Blanca to have a good time and you challenge me to a gunfight!

"They say my world is the Planet X. From my experience, I think your planet is the real Planet X!

"Today is my first day on your planet and I'm thinking I should put my guns back on before I get killed. At this rate, I may not make it two days here! I felt safe with my guns on in Tombstone but I'm not allowed to carry a gun on your planet."

Chad asks, "How are the women on Earth, Gunnar?"

"I like the women here a lot better. The women on my world have their noses up in the air. They could touch the top of a building with those noses. Some will not even say 'Hi' unless they want something. And if you help her, next week she won't say 'Hi' to you again.

"There was a woman I used to know from work—Gina. She was good to talk to so I asked her out for pizza and beer. She said Monday would be good but didn't know what time so I gave her my number and told her to call me that night. That was Saturday. She didn't. The next day at work I thought she would say something. But she didn't. Monday, I washed my truck for that night (a truck is kind of like a conductor—it takes you where you want to go). She could have called me at anytime because I have a cell phone. But she did not call me on Monday either and I did not have her number to call her.

"So the next day Gina said, 'I'm so sorry I didn't call you.'

"I told her, 'It was my mistake for asking you out.'

"As time went by, we started talking again. The normal subject of beer came up again and she said, 'A beer sounds good right now.'

"I said, 'You had your chance.'

"She told me, 'Sorry about that, Gunnar.'

95

"I said, 'Fine. Would you still like to go out?'

"She said, 'Yes, I would like that. I think I'm free on Monday.'

"I told her, 'You have my phone number, call and let me know.'

"As I walked off I thought, 'What have I done? God, not again!'

"I knew I wouldn't hear from her. That was Saturday. No phone call that night. The next day she didn't say a word about not phoning. On Monday, I didn't wash my dirty truck because I knew she was not going to call me—and I was right.

"The next day she said, 'Sorry I didn't call. I lost your number.' She could have said something on Sunday at work! But I was not mad since I knew she was not going to call me anyway.

"That's women for you on my world.

"There are some good women but they're hard to find. You know that if you live there. There is one at my church who says 'Hi' to me. She's a good person.

"Some men on my world will not marry a woman because of the way they are. Other men just live with women but don't marry them. That way they can go anytime they want to.

"One minute they're happy. The next minute they're mad at you. Then they say you don't understand them."

One of the cowgirls is named Claudia. She says, "I'm not like that but I know others girl who are. I like to be good to a man all the time and I make sure he knows it."

We talk and laugh and drink more beer for some time.

Eventually, it's getting late so I say, "It's been fun talking to you all but I have to go."

Chad says, "I like you, human, you are okay."

"I like you, too," Claudia tells me.

"The feeling is mutual," I respond.

What a nice body Claudia has. I find myself taking her clothes off with my eyes. That's what Jack said he likes to do, too.

Noticing this, she asks me, "May I hug you?"

"Yes, if you want to."

She feels so damn good in my arms.

"Will I see you again, Earthman?" Chad asks.

"I don't know. We will see.

"Blanca, let's head out."

I wave goodbye to Toby.

"You come back here again," he says, "and drinks will always be on the house for you, Earthman."

As Blanca and I walk outside, she asks, "Do you want to come to my home, Gunnar, and just talk?"

"It's kind of late, don't you think?"

"A bit," she says. "Spend some time with *me* now—alone."

"Well, okay. For a little while."

She takes out her conductor and holds my hand. Instantly, we are outside of her house.

"Come on in, Gunnar. Don't be frightened of me."

"It's quite pretty in here in your home. I love your furniture."

"Sit here by me," she says. "Would you like something to drink?"

"A glass of water would be good right now."

She brings it and sits next to me.

"Are you happy with me, Gunnar?"

"Yes, you know I am, Blanca. You're my kind of woman."

She moves closer and asks, "Can I kiss you, Gunnar?"

"Yes, that's okay with me."

I put my arm around her and start to kiss her lips and face.

She says, "Do not stop. I like that—with your hands all over me. I like you so much, Gunnar. Do you want to go to bed with me?"

I back away and say, "I like you but we've had too much to drink. That makes people do things they normally won't do. In the morning, you're going to ask yourself why you did what you did. I should go. I'm only a human from Planet X. You know we're like animals."

I pull out my conductor as she unbuttons her dress in front of me and pleads, "Don't go. Please stay and I'll make you feel like you've never felt before with a woman down there on Earth."

97

"It's better this way," I tell her. "You'll see in the morning."

A second later, I'm back home.

So close yet so far…

What a woman! I cannot believe I just walked away from that! I'll always remember her as the one I let slip away. Still, I only got lucky because I said 'No.' It's so hard to be good when you've got a woman like that in front of you. But that's life. I'm going to bed now all alone when I could have been with Blanca by my side.

In the morning, I use my conductor to go to John's home.

John shouts, "Come on in, Gunnar. The door is open."

I go in and greet John and Karen.

She asks, "How was last night with Blanca?"

"It was okay," I respond. "I do like her. She is so nice of a person. "You know, John, the people here look so young and full of life."

"How old do you think I am?" he asks.

"I'm not good at guessing ages but I'd say you're about fifty."

"No, you are far from right. I am one hundred and ten years old."

"No way! How can that be?"

"Come over here. See this box? On top is a computer. You simply tell it the age that you are and how old you want to look. I would say the average age here is about one-hundred and fifty."

"How old can you get to be?"

"Up to about four hundred years. We really watch what we eat.

"Do you want to be younger again, Gunnar? It only takes an hour. We could easily take five or ten years off you."

"Naw, people know me as I am. Time can't take that away. I look like me and I'm happy with myself."

"It's your choice," he says.

"By the way, John, how old is Blanca?"

John looks at me and says, "Gunnar, on your world you never ask any woman her age. You know that. The same applies here. However, I will state this—*take it to your heart, not to your eyes.* Love is very tough to find. It is tougher to find than gold. But when you find love, it means much more than life itself. You have seen gold but you have also seen a woman's eyes. If you only listen, her eyes will talk to you, while the gold cannot. Some claim that gold is worth a lot of money. But love is free and worth a lot more. You have touched real gold and you have touched a woman's hand. The truth—which is worth more? How old is gold and how old is a woman? Who cares—as long as you are in love with her. That love is worth much more than anything on any world if you have it. Don't lose it my friend."

"I understand, John."

"Anyway," he continues, "Your time machine is ready to go."

"I didn't know it was broken," I tell him. "By the way—why do your people repair my time machine when it breaks down?"

"Do you really know what you have there?" he asks. "We repair it for you so nobody else will get their hands on it there on Earth.

"There's no reason we couldn't just take it from you but it is yours now and not ours anymore. That would be stealing it, which is against the law here. How could we tell others that it is wrong to steal if we, ourselves, are thieves? The law is not just for some but for all people, even if on your world, some obey it and some don't.

"I would like to show you something on your time machine now."

We walk back to where the time machine is parked.

"Under the steering wheel is a button. Press it and within an area of twenty-five feet around the time machine, if you were underwater, you could go out and will not get wet. If you go to another planet and the air is bad, you will still be protected if you want to go outside.

"Next to that is another button. If you push it, people will see you. You will basically be a 'UFO' to them.

"But be careful. On your world, especially in Russia, they will try to shoot you down. They have shot down other time machines before but the pilots were able to completely self-destruct first. Those pilots died to keep this technology away from the Russians. And so if you push this other button here, you will also be gone for good.

"Between the two bucket seats is a box. See these two levers that look like emergency brakes? At the end of each is a button. This one closest to you fires laser bullets which can go through four-inch steel. The other lever fires a laser-guided bomb which can destroy an entire building in a single shot. With these, if you're ever attacked, you now have something to fight back with.

"Oh, and if you ever encounter a race called the *Gettion* you must kill them or they will kill you. They often go to Earth and abduct your people. They have killed many of your kind. Your government knows but says nothing since they cannot stop them. Your people would be terrified if they knew how helpless your government really is."

"That is very disturbing.

"I think it's time to go home now.

"Karen, say 'Goodbye' to Blanca for me."

"I will."

"You know," I remark to John, "it occurred to me that 'Blanca' is a Spanish name..."

"Did it not occur to you that 'John' is an Earth name, too?"

"Well, now that you mention it..."

"The fact is, like the rest of our language, our real names would be unpronounceable to you. The language computer simply translates our Antonion names into equivalent Earth names."

"That makes sense. She looks like a 'Blanca.'"

"Which means I look like a "John.'"

"Anyway, thank you for everything."

He asks, "What are you going to do about the black man?"

"Nothing."

"Why?"

"The North was against enslaving people but the South was not. We went to war because of the back man and many died because of it. If I stop the white man from bringing the black man over from Africa there will have been no war and my history will be changed—good or bad, I do not know. But I'll let it be for now."

"You are smart for a human. Don't let anyone tell you otherwise.

"I hope you come back someday so we can talk some more. See those other buttons over there? That one will take you home to Earth. That one next to it is programmed to take you back here to Antonion."

He then goes into his pocket and takes out a wristwatch and hands it to me. "This is for you. It keeps good time, all the time."

"Oh, thank you."

"In your country, you will go to different states with different time zones. With this watch, you won't have to keep updating the time.

"And see this button on top? Each time you push it, time will slow down more and more until it completely stops. So if you get in a fight, just press it and that other person will slow down while you still move normally. You will then always win the fight. Nobody will ever know what happened."

"That should come in handy."

"Good luck and goodbye for now," John says.

I shake his hand and give Karen a hug.

I get into my time machine, push the button for home and take off.

I can now see their entire planet from high in the sky.

Boy, this machine can go very fast now!

Theodore Aguilera

Chapter 9: **A Matter of Money**

I'm approaching Earth…

Down I go…

The outside of the time machine is red-hot and on fire. However, the inside remains nice and cool.

The first thing I need to do is get to the hospital and see my best friend, Tom, who is dying of cancer.

I see a place to park my craft. I put her down slowly.

I get out and make my way into the hospital.

Arriving at Tom's room, I see him lying in bed. He does not look too good to me.

"Hi, Tom. What's new with you today?"

"Hey, Gunnar. The same old thing—I'm dying here, you know. What about you?"

"Well, I went to another world, drank some beer there, met a lot of pretty women who wanted me for improper sex—you know how women are—only thinking about sex. I said 'No, thank you.'"

"You always could tell a good story, Gunnar."

"Oh, and on that planet I talked to one of their doctors. I told him about you and your cancer and how the doctors here can't do a damn thing about it. He told me to just give you one of these pills and your cancer will be gone. What do you say about that? Here you go."

"What is this?—really…"

"Just take the damn pill and your cancer will be gone. Or, you can die—it's up to you. You know me, Tom. We've been best friends for a long time now. I believe the doctor."

Tom looks carefully at the pill in my hand.

"Well, do you want the pill or not?" I ask. "To get out of that bed and get well and get out of this damn hospital?"

"What do I have to lose?" he says. "I'm dying anyway. Give me the damn pill and get me some water."

"Remember, though," I tell him, "the doctor there told me not to tell anybody on our world about this."

"Did you really go to another world? Tell me the truth."

"Yes, I did. And one day I will take you there, too, so you can see it for yourself."

Tom finally takes the pill.

"Good," I say. "I'll see you later. I have to go now."

I head out to my time machine and hop in. I set it for two weeks in the future and push the launch button.

Two weeks go by in an instant.

I go back into the hospital and into Tom's room. A doctor is there. He says to Tom, "You are a lucky man. Your cells are fighting off the cancer. I don't know how this is, but you're going to live."

The doctor leaves the room, shaking his head.

"Gunnar!" Tom shouts, "That pill worked like you said it would!"

"Yes, I know. The doctor from the other planet told me."

"I'll be okay now, because of you—my best friend."

"I will always be your best friend, Tom."

"We'll have to go out and have some beer—I'm buying," he says. "I will buy all you can drink, Gunnar."

"I hope you have a lot of money because I do drink a lot of beer," I tell him. "I'll see you later. Take care and get some rest."

I head out to my time machine to run a few errands. I need to go to the bank and get enough money to live on while I travel around this world of ours and see new places.

I get to the bank where many people are standing in line.

When finally my turn, I say to the teller, "I would like to close my account, please."

She responds, "You have three-thousand, two-hundred dollars and thirty cents in your account now, sir. How do you want it?"

"I'll need some ones, fives, tens, twenties, fifties and hundreds."

She pays me and I put all my money in my pocket.

I'm about ready to leave as two armed men enter the bank.

They yell for everyone to cooperate or be shot.

One of the robbers sees a pretty woman. He kisses her and says, "You're coming home with me. I'm going to have you all night long in my bed and you will like it, baby."

A police officer walks in; not knowing the bank is being robbed.

One of the gunmen shoots the officer, who had done nothing.

That does it for me.

I push my ring and everyone stops. I walk over to the gunmen and take all the bullets from their guns. I then go back to the police officer and take the gun from his holster.

I then push my ring and the people start to move again.

The men see me with the policeman and his gun in my hand. They try to open fire against me with their empty guns.

I point my gun at them and they decide to set their guns down.

I ask them, "Why did you murder that policeman?"

One of them responds, "I don't know—Sorry for that we did..."

I tell them, "How you would like it if I shot you?"

"No!" he begs, "I wouldn't like it at all!"

"But," I say, "You did try to shoot me, didn't you?"

The man who shot the policeman says, "Look, man, it's nothing personal! We're sorry already! What more can we do? It's done!"

I say, "I do believe you that you are sorry for shooting at me."

I then shoot him in the shoulder and the other man, too.

They fall to the ground as the women start to scream.

I tell the men, "I'm so sorry I did that. Please forgive me, sirs."

I hear police sirens growing louder in the distance.

The man that shot the policeman screams out, "You're nuts, man! You shot us! What's wrong with you, man?"

"That is true—I do like shooting people I don't like," I tell them. "I am a little nuts but I like it and I have the gun."

I shoot his foot. "I'm so sorry I did that. I am just a little bit nuts. Please forgive me again."

I walk to the pretty woman and give her the gun. I tell her, "If they move even a little, just shoot them."

She points the handgun at the man that kissed her and says, "I'll definitely shoot that one. You can count on it."

The man stares at the gun barrel she has pointed at him.

I tell one of the customers to go outside and bring in the police.

I tell everybody to turn away. I then push my ring and time around me stops. My time machine appears and I get in and close the door. Everyone starts moving again.

The police enter and begin looking for me but I head out through a wall and leave the scene.

Soon, I land my craft by the building of a nearby coin dealer.

I walk into the store.

A man there asks, "Can I help you?"

"I'm look for some money from 1956. Can you help me?"

"Yes, I can help you. Take a look at these."

"How much are they?"

"Well, sir, this one-dollar bill costs ten dollars today. This twenty-dollar bill is one hundred dollars. Not a bad deal for you today, sir."

"I have a good friend named Jack. He knows a lot about bills and coins. Perhaps you have dealt with him?"

"Ah," he says. "He travels all over the world. He had a lot of stock which he sold for a lot of money. Once he was poor, now he is a very rich man and has a beautiful woman."

"I think my friend is the same man you are talking about."

"So would you like to buy some money here?"

"Yes, I would. I need about a hundred dollars. I want some ones, tens and twenty-dollar bills."

"Here you are, sir. That will be three-hundred dollars. I gave you a good deal because you are a friend of Jack."

I pay the man and ask, "Do you have a bag I could have?"

"Yes, I do. It's on the house for you, sir."

"Thanks," I say to him. "If you see Jack again, say 'Hello' for me. Say it's from Gunnar Best."

"I will, sir. Good day."

I walk outside to my time machine and get in. I set the date for 1956 at 10:00 am. I'm off to San Francisco…

I can see the Golden Gate Bridge from here up in the sky.

I'm now over the Federal Building.

I slowly set my time machine down near it.

As the glow of its skin fades, I open the door and climb out.

I walk inside the Federal building and take the elevator to the floor where the FBI is listed in the lobby.

A man sits at reception. I ask him, "Can I see a person here about counterfeit bills?"

"Can I see your ID, please?" he asks. He glances at it and picks up his phone, dials and begins talking into it. He then hangs up and says, "Please take this guest ID tag and put it on."

I do so and he directs me down the hall where he says somebody will meet with me.

In one of the offices I pass, I see a woman and man standing there looking at me with polite smiles on their faces.

I stop, look back and smile at them, too.

The woman is dressed in a white suit and is very pretty for an FBI agent. The man is dressed in a back suit. He is about forty years old.

He says, "I'm Agent Daniels. This is Agent Alley. Please come in and sit here so we can talk."

I take a seat facing them.

"You want to talk about counterfeit bills—is that right?" he asks.

Looking at a picture of the current American President—Dwight David Eisenhower—on the wall, I say "Yes, it's my money, you see."

"What do you mean?" Agent Alley asks.

"It's a bit hard to explain but I'll do my best. Just let me talk first and when I'm done you can ask me any questions. Is that okay?"

"Go ahead and we'll listen, sir," Daniels says.

"Well—I am from the future. I know that's hard to believe right now but it's the truth. I am from the year 2010."

Daniels says to Alley, "I don't have time for this. You want me to tell this man where to go?"

"No, it's okay. I'll listen to him," she responds.

Daniels tells her, "I'll see you later…"

"Please go ahead with your story, sir," she says.

Daniels walks out and closes the door.

"Thank you, Agent Alley, for listening. I went to a coin dealer in 2010 for some money from this time period. I asked for one hundred dollars but had to pay him three hundred for it.

"Well, I thought if I came here to the FBI, you would understand that American money should still be good at any time, right?"

"Yes, it is as good tomorrow as it is today."

"Agent Alley, I was in 1914, drinking beer with a friend. I wanted to pay but he said I couldn't because my money was from the future."

"Do you have some of that money from the future with you here?"

"I have two-thousand, nine-hundred dollars in this bag. I took the money out from my bank account today in 2010—about an hour ago."

Alley asks, "Can I see it?"

"Yes. In fact, it's yours if I can exchange it for the same currency of this time period." I hand it over to her and she begins inspecting it.

"It looks a lot different…" she comments.

"I didn't make it myself, of course. Our government did.

"You see, I only have one hundred dollars from this period. If you can't help, I'll have to go back to that coin dealer in my time. You can save me a lot of money if you can."

I see her eyes opening wide as she looks up and down at the bills. "These look authentic! I have never seen money like this before. I will need to speak to someone before I can say anything. Please wait here. I'll be right back, Mr.—what is your name, sir?"

"My name is Gunnar Best."

"I'll be right back Mr. Best."

She takes my money and walks out, leaving the door open a little.

I can hear her talking to a man down the hall. She tells him of my claim of being from the future and shows him my money from 2010.

He asks, "What did Agent Daniels say about this?"

"He just left the room after Mr. Best brought up time traveling."

"I see."

"Sir, this man wants to know if he can trade his money for ours."

"We need more time, Agent. Have him stay at a hotel for tonight. Tell him we'll pay for his stay.

"And you tell that Daniels to get his ass in my office right now."

"Yes, sir."

I hear her walking back.

She stops and I hear her softly say, "Agent Marcus wants to talk to you right now."

Agent Daniels' voice can be heard asking, "About what?"

"Go find out for yourself."

"By the way," he asks, "what about that crazy man from the future you were talking to? Is he still here?"

"Yes he is…"

Agent Alley walks in.

"Mr. Best, my superior needs more time to look over your money. He asks that you stay at a hotel—on us. We'll take you if you want."

"Okay, I guess."

"I'll just make the arrangements and will be right back," she tells me as she walks out of the room.

I hear Agent Marcus on his phone. "Mint Office?—Agent Marcus. I want your best man on counterfeit bills in my office who can tell me if this money I have is real or not. Not tomorrow but today."

Daniels walks in his office and asks, "You asked to see me, sir?"

"Daniels, why did you walk out on that man?"

"Sir, he spoke of time traveling… He was obviously crazy."

"Did you even see the money he had on him?"

"I don't know anything about any money."

"Take a look," Marcus says. "Now tell me why you left."

"I've never seen bills like these before," Daniels remarks.

"And you just assumed he was a crazy man and left Agent Alley to deal with him alone. What if he *is* a time traveler from the future and he does have a time machine?—and you just let him walk out... I'm just happy that Agent Alley was there to talk to this man or he'd be gone for good. She'll take care of this case from here. Now get out of my office. I don't want to see your face again today. You hear?"

"Yes, sir," Daniels nervously replies.

Agent Alley walks in and asks, "Are you ready to go, Mr. Best?"

"Yes, I am."

We walk out to the parking lot. I hop in the backseat of a car with Agent Alley next to me as another man drives us away.

We stop in front of the hotel and are let out.

With Agent Alley by my side, I take note of how nice this hotel really is as the doorman lets us in.

Arriving at the counter, Agent Alley says, "Mr. Best is a guest of the FBI. Whatever Mr. Best wants, please see that he gets it."

"Yes, of course, ma'am," the gentleman behind the desk says.

The bellhop approaches the counter and the receptionist tells him, "Take Mr. Best to room 407 right away please."

"Come this way please," he says.

We go to my room and I am amazed at how big and beautiful it is.

Agent Alley hands me her card and tells me, "If you need me for anything, please give me a call—anytime, day or night, Mr. Best."

"This may not be right to ask of an FBI agent—but would you like to have a drink with me in the hotel bar?"

"I would like that very much, Mr. Best."

We walk down to the bar and find a good table by the window.

The waiter arrives and asks, "Is there anything I can start you off with today?"

"Yes," I reply, "a beer for me, please."

"I'll have a beer, too," she says.

"I'll be right back with your drinks."

After bringing us our glasses, I pick mine up and think to myself, "Here's to the fine women of 1956. I drink to them and their beauty."

Debbie asks, "Is your time machine in a secure place? If not, I can see to it that it is."

"Please, call me Gunnar."

"Alright, Gunnar. You can call me Debbie if you like."

"Thank you.

"And yes, it is very safe. No one can find it."

A man across the restaurant watches us. I know he's an FBI agent. I say to Debbie, "It's nice to know that you and I are not alone today."

"What do you mean?"

"Over there is another FBI agent watching us. He's good. I didn't even see him at first."

She asks, "Do you want him to go away?"

"It's okay. He's doing his job."

"So what are you going to do with your money?" she asks.

"Go look around the city and see if there's anything I might take back to my time. Maybe I'll get lucky and meet a nice woman here. I never know what will happen next."

She asks, "What do you like best about the time you live in?"

"I'd say my phone is my favorite thing of all. I love my phone."

"I have a phone, too, but I can't say I love it. It's just a phone."

"But, Debbie, your phone is from 1956 while mine is from 2010. If someone calls and you're not home, what can you do? In my time, if you phone me and I'm not home, I can still talk to you."

"How?"

"I'll show you."

I take out my cell phone and place it on the table.

She looks at it.

The waiter comes and asks, "How are we doing here? Would you like another beer, sir?"

"Let's have other round," I tell him.

The waiter nods and leaves.

"Anyway," I say, "that is my phone from the future."

"Can I look at it?"

"Yes, you can."

She picks it up and inspects it. "It's so small for a phone."

The waiter comes with our two beers and asks, "Could you please sign here, sir?"

I sign it and he thanks me and walks away.

"You know, Debbie, I was on another planet and I paid my bill by putting my hand on a computer. It took the money out of my account for me. Here on this planet I have to sign."

"You've been on another world?"

"Yes. Good people live out there."

"Your phone looks like a little toy to me."

"Would you like to talk to my brother with this 'toy' of mine?"

"Does your brother live here in the city?"

"No, and he lives in the future in 2010. How about that?"

"Okay, then I would like to talk to your brother."

I take back my phone and begin punching in James' number.

I explain, "Despite the fact that my brother and I are in a different space and time, this phone can work across both...

"Hi, James. I am here talking with a pretty woman from the FBI. Would you like to speak with her? Her name is Debbie."

"Sure," he says. "I always have time to talk to a pretty lady!"

I give her my phone and she says "Hello there..." into it.

James responds, "Hello, how are you doing over there?"

"Fine. What year is it over there?"

"2010—why?" he asks.

"Because over here, it's 1956."

"Looks like my brother's doing some more time traveling."

"It would seem so. Your brother is very nice."

"Well, you don't know my brother like I do!"

I ask Debbie, "Can I please have my phone back?"

She hands me my phone and I say to James, "Okay, I have to go."

"Oh!" he says, "A hot chick came by. She said you told her it was okay to visit. She said she was washing her car when you met."

"Oh yeah! I've got one thing to say to you, brother—she's *mine,* not *yours*—you remember that."

"Don't worry, I'll show her a good time for you."

"Goodbye, James. Take care of yourself."

"Well," I tell her, "that was James. He's a pretty cool brother.

"Here—let me take your picture with my phone. Is that okay?"

"Your phone can take my picture, too?"

"Sure!"

I raise my phone and take two pictures of her and show them to her on its screen. She stares at them and says, "I cannot believe it. No phone in our time can do that!

"Would you like to show me your time machine, Gunnar?"

"No, I'd like to, but not right now. In time, maybe. We'll see."

"Well, I have to be going," she says. "I have to get back to work."

"Okay, I'll see you later."

As she walks out, I head to the bar and sit. I say to the bartender, "How's it going with you, sir?"

"It's going okay," he replies.

We engage in a little small-talk before the most beautiful woman I have ever seen comes in and sits next to me. She's wearing a low-cut dress and it looks great on her.

She says, "Hi there, big boy. How are you doing?"

I find it hard to say 'Hi' to a woman like that. I just say, "okay."

She tells me, "I like your tan. It looks sexy on you."

"Oh, thank you."

She says, "You must have a lot of girlfriends with that tan."

"No," I say, "I don't have a girl now but I'm always looking."

The bartender looks at me knowing that I'm getting lucky tonight.

She says, "I just saw you with a pretty woman. She's not yours?"

"No, she works for the FBI."

"Oh… Do you mind telling me what you talked about?"

"I have some money, you see, and she's just going to exchange it for some new money. That's all."

"You could go to any bank and do that," she says.

"No, not this money. Only she can do this for me."

"Did she bring you to this hotel?"

"Yeah."

"She just left you all alone with so many other women?" she asks. "You can never tell what they may do to you here…"

"Yeah. The FBI is paying for it all, too. Even my drinks and food. In fact, let me buy you a drink."

"That would be nice of you."

"Well, the FBI's paying for it."

"You are a good-looking man," she tells me.

"Could you do me a favor?"

"Yes," she says. "Anything—here or upstairs…"

"Over by the door, a man is watching us. Would you mind waving him away?"

She gives a faint smile and waves at the FBI agent to go.

The man gets up and leaves.

I then ask her, "Who do you work for—the FBI?"

She responds, "Yes. It's my job to make you happy and get you to talk to me. You and I could have had a good time together."

"With you, yes, but not with the FBI. Goodbye, young lady."

She walks away.

I ask the bartender, "Do you have a phone I could use?"

"Yes, sir."

Placing it on the bar, I call Agent Alley. I ask her, "Did you send a beautiful woman here to get information out of me?"

"No, of course not."

"Well, this woman told me she worked for the FBI. How many FBI agencies do we have here in this city?"

"How did you know? What did you tell her?"

"Debbie, she was just too nice to me. I knew something was up. She was totally hitting on me and she looked too good. I only told her that I was sorry but she had to go."

"I'll look into it, Gunnar."

Half an hour goes by before Agent Alley calls me back.

Her story was this:

After speaking to me on the phone, she went into her superior's office and asked, "Sir, who sent that woman to Mr. Best at the hotel?"

"I don't know what you're talking about."

"Someone sent a woman there to get information out of him."

He then yelled out, "Get Agent Daniels in here right now!"

Daniels arrived and Marcus asked him about the woman.

"Yes, I sent her," Daniels confessed.

"Didn't I say Agent Alley would take care of Mr. Best, herself?"

"Yes, but I thought this would be more effective."

Debbie shouted, "Now he doesn't want to talk to us at all!"

She then went on to describe the phone in my pocket that had no wires and how she used it to speak to my brother in 2010. She also explained how I took her picture with my phone as well.

"Impossible!" Agent Daniels cried. "No one can take your picture with a phone! I don't believe it."

Agent Marcus cut in with, "Men from the Mint Office were here. One of them said he never seen bills like this in his thirty years there. I asked if they were counterfeit. He said they were very real but could not explain how they were made. He kept going on about wanting to see more of this 2010 technology and how he wanted to meet this man from the future and go there himself.

"Daniels, what do you think of Mr. Best?"

"I don't know, sir. I left the room after we met."

"What do you think of this man, Agent Alley?"

"He's nice. He likes to talk about time travel a lot."

"Do you think he'll let me talk to him about it?"

"Well, he's a bit mistrusting of us after today."

While they spoke, there was a knock at the door. A man from the CIA came in with some questions. He was Agent Roberts. He wore a brown suit and a blue shirt with a brown tie.

He said, "I understand we have a time traveler in our midst?"

Marcus told him that this matter was none of his business.

Roberts said, "We're on the same side, are we not? I heard about a man who might need some money—about three-thousand dollars. Is that not true? If you don't have the money maybe I can help here."

"No," Debbie told him, "he belongs to us."

"Is he a person or a thing? Do you own papers on him?"

"You know what I'm talking about, Roberts."

"Why not let the man make up his own mind? You don't have to tell me that he's in a hotel downtown if you don't want to."

Marcus said, "We are having a little problem with Mr. Best at the moment. He's angry with us."

"Well, he's not mad at me. He's only mad at you, the FBI. We're lucky I came in time to save the day."

"He likes me," Debbie said. "I can talk to him for you if you want. It could be good or it could be bad but he knows me better than you."

Roberts replied, "I have a great idea. We can work together. After all, like I said, we're on the same side, are we not?"

Back in the bar, the bartender says, "She was a beautiful woman, mister. I'd leave my wife for that in a second—no question about it. She was hot. My wife is not. That will be the last beautiful woman in here tonight, you can count on it."

I chuckle a little.

But after five minutes, yet another beautiful woman walks in and she's looking at me.

I get up and walk around to the other side of the bar and sit down.

Nevertheless, she still comes on over and sits beside me.

She says, "Can I sit here with you?"

I look at the bartender and he looks at me. I can see in this eyes a look of, "You are the luckiest man on Earth."

This woman has blonde hair, blue eyes and red lips which could touch mine anytime she wants them to. She also has a hot red dress that is so tight on her, I could die.

She asks, "What's your name?"

"Gunnar. And you are?"

"Candy. You do like candy, don't you?"

"Yes, it tastes so good on your lips…"

I get up and go to the jukebox and play some music.

A man walks in, sits in my chair and starts talking to Candy.

I sit on the other side of the bar away from them.

Candy says to the man, "I am with that man over there."

He gets up, walks over to me and sits. He looks at me and asks, "Is she with you?—yes or no?"

"She's not with me."

"Would you fight for a woman like that?"

That's it. I get up, walk to the other side of the bar and sit down. I say to the bartender, "One more beer, please."

Candy goes to the man and tells him to "get the hell out of here." She then comes to me and asks, "Why didn't you help me with him?"

"Well, young lady, I'm just sitting here having a beer. That's it. I'm not going to fight for a woman I don't know."

"I like you, Gunnar. I just want to sit with you and have a drink."

The bartender looks at me with a grin on his face, knowing that I will be getting lucky tonight.

I look into her eyes and say, "Can I ask you something? Which do you work for, the FBI or the CIA?"

She responds, "The CIA."

"Now we can have a good time. Let's sit over at that table."

Maybe I will get lucky tonight.

"So what's your name," I ask, "—your *real* name?"

117

"Terry. And your name is Gunnar Best. They told me at the office to get you to talk to me. Why?"

"Well, Terry, it's a long story but it's because I am a time traveler. I'm from the future—the year 2010.

"You are a beautiful woman—any man can see that. I could like a woman like you very easily. But women like you do not like men like me in my time. Women like you only go after men with money and I have no money. That makes it hard to talk to a woman like you."

"I might be beautiful on the outside, nevertheless, on the inside I am still a person—a human being like you."

The bartender comes with two beers.

I say, "It's nice to sit with a beautiful woman and talk to her."

"Do you have a girlfriend in your time?"

"Not right now. I do like this woman who lives in 1914. She is so pretty and nice to talk to but she's not perfect. She has her faults."

Debbie walks in with a man I do not know. She sees me drinking with this beautiful woman and asks me, "How are you doing here?"

"I am doing fine. This is Terry. Terry, this is Debbie. Terry works for the CIA. She wants me to talk to her about my time machine, too."

Debbie says, "This is Agent Roberts. He also works for the CIA. He is not nearly as pretty as Terry but would also like to talk to you about your time machine, if possible."

"How would you like to see my time machine right now?"

"Yes," he says, "I would like that very much."

"I was just joking, Roberts. You like to joke around don't you?

He laughs and says, "Yes, I do, Gunnar."

I say, "I am so happy you came here when you did, Roberts. I was just going to show Terry my time machine and take her back to have some beer with me in 1914 and meet a good friend of mine there."

Roberts says, "With that machine you can make a lot of money."

I respond, "Agent Roberts, if our Government gave me a million dollars, I'd probably be left with only five hundred after taxes.

"I'm going to my room now alone because of you, Agent Roberts.

"It has been fun, Terry. We would have had a good time in 1914 but not today thanks to him."

I walk back to my room, alone.

It's a big room with a big bed but nobody to sleep with in it.

What a woman that was! Damn it.

I push my ring.

The time machine appears there in my room.

I start putting my things inside, like my phone and conductor.

I see my gun in the trunk. I pat it and smile at my old friend.

I push my ring again and the time machine is gone.

The next morning, Debbie and Agent Roberts knock on my door.

I tell them to come in.

I say to Roberts, "I forgive you for ruining my night with Terry."

"Oh, good."

"Gunnar," Debby says, "can you come to the FBI office today?"

"Yes, but let me have breakfast first. It's very important to me."

"You can order here in your room," Roberts says.

"No, let's go down to the restaurant. I'd like to see the people of 1956. Is that okay with you?"

We head downstairs. I see a good table. We sit.

The waiter arrives and asks, "What would you like today?"

I tell him, "I'd like coffee and a piece of pie—any pie will do."

Roberts says, "Just coffee for me."

Debbie orders the same.

The waiter acknowledges us and scurries off.

"Did you sleep well last night?" Debbie asks.

"Yes. However, it could have been better…" Roberts and I look at each other without saying a word.

The waiter comes with our coffee and my pie.

I ask the waiter, "How much is the coffee here?"

"It's a bit high here at twenty-five cents a cup."

"That's a decent price," I say. "Not bad at all for a cup of coffee. Where I live, I pay a dollar ninety."

"No!" the waiter responds.

"Yes, I do!"

"Where is that, sir?"

"In the future. Not too far from here, actually."

He looks at me as if I told a bad joke.

"Heck," I continue, "at the airport the same coffee is five dollars!"

Roberts tells the waiter, "He's just joking. Please go, young man."

The waiter leaves.

Roberts says to me, "You shouldn't say things like that to people."

"You're right, Agent Roberts. I will not talk about time travel or time machines to anybody anymore—to the FBI, the CIA or to you."

Debbie gives Roberts a dirty look.

I tell him, "I can say anything I want to anyone I want. You're not my mother or my wife. I came to your time alone and I'll leave alone. Goodbye, Agents Alley and Roberts."

I get up and start walking away.

Debbie says, "You don't have to go. Please, let's sit over there."

I turn and say to her, "I'll miss you, Debbie. It's been fun. I'll see you at the FBI building."

As I walk away, I hear her saying to Roberts, "I thought you came to save the day, not to destroy it."

Debbie catches up with me and says, "Sorry about that, Gunnar. We can take you there if you want us to."

"No, I may say something wrong again with Agent Roberts there. I better go alone but thank you anyway.

"Debbie, you are a good friend. I thought you should know that. But not him."

I stop a taxi and tell him to take me to the Federal Building.

After getting there, I enter the large structure and see a man sitting at reception. I ask to see Agent Alley about some counterfeit bills.

"What is your name, sir?"

"Gunnar Best."

"Go in, Mr. Best. She's actually away now but will be back soon. Here is your ID. Just head through those two doors."

I enter Debbie's office and find a man standing there.

He says, "My name is Agent Doug Marcus. Come in Mr. Best."

He shakes my hand.

Debbie and Roberts walk in.

Marcus asks, "You already know these people, don't you?"

"Yes, I do."

"Please sit down," Marcus says. "Would you like some coffee?"

"No, thank you.

"Is my money okay with you people?"

Marcus responds, "I would like you to meet someone." He sticks his head out of the office and waves for someone to come in. "This is Mr. David Peterson. He works for the Mint Office. He has seen your money and says it looks authentic to him."

Peterson says, "I'm intrigued by your money, Mr. Best. Please tell me more about the future you come from."

"No, I will not talk about the future to you or anyone else. Agent Roberts here told me not to."

"I did say that," Roberts responds, "however, only because he was talking about it to a waiter."

"What's the difference between David here and a waiter?" I ask. "You're both human beings, are you not?"

"Yes," David says, "but I work for the government."

I respond, "And he works for the restaurant—big deal.

"If the money is okay, can I exchange it and go?"

David says, "I have a lot of questions for you first about your time machine and the future that will come to us all."

"No. Give me your money or my money and I'll be on my way."

David says, "Okay—here is the money, straight from the mint."

"Well, thank you and goodbye," I tell them. "By the way, Roberts, you don't have that beautiful woman's number on you do you?"

"No, I do not."

"I thought I'd ask her out one day but thanks anyway."

I begin my departure from the Federal Building.

I hear Roberts asking, "You're going to let him go just like that?"

"We can't hold him," Marcus says. "We have no cause."

Roberts says, "This is unacceptable. I still have many questions to ask about his time machine and the future."

I exit the building and make my way to the bus station.

From there, I hop on a bus to Berkeley.

After the short trip, I get off and see a man selling hotdogs on the street. I buy a couple and a Coke. I then go sit on the grass and eat.

A police officer passes and asks, "What are you doing here?"

"I'm eating a hot dog."

"What's in your bag there?"

"Money."

"Is it yours?"

"Yes, of course."

"Can you prove it?"

"No, it's cash. But I know it's mine."

"Let's see your money right now," he demands.

I hand it to him. He looks it over and says, "You're under arrest. Come with me right now."

"For what?"

"You know for what," he barks. "Don't play games with me, boy, or you're just gunna get hurt. You understand me?"

We get to the police station and stop at the front desk.

He says to the sergeant there, "I got the man whose been robbing all those stores around town. Look at all this money he had on him. Looks like about three-thousand dollars."

"I think you got our man," the sergeant says. "We've been looking for him a long time now."

"But this is *my* money!" I shout.

"Then where did you get it?" the officer asks.

"I got it from the FBI. They gave it to me."

The officer hits me in the face and yells, "That's for lying to me you asshole! Why would the FBI give you all that money?"

"I gave them three-thousand dollars first and they gave me three-thousand dollars back."

The officer then punches me again. "That's for lying to me again. Don't you ever learn? Can you believe this guy?"

"Lock him up!" the sergeant says, "I don't want to see his face."

"I get a phone call don't I?"

"Give him the phone," the sergeant says in disgust.

I take out Debbie's card and dial her number. "Agent Alley? It's Gunnar Best. I'm in jail in Berkeley. Can you come and get me out?"

"Jail? I'll be there right away."

Thirty minutes later, I watch Debbie and Roberts arriving through the bars of my cell. Debbie says, "We want to talk about a man you're holding. His name is Gunnar Best."

Roberts says, "Can we see his belongings first, please?"

"Who the hell are you?" the sergeant asks.

"I am Agent Alley from the Federal Bureau of Investigation." She holds up her badge.

"I'm Agent Roberts from the CIA." He shows his badge, too.

The sergeant yells, "Who the hell is this man we got?"

Debbie responds, "His name is Gunnar Best. The FBI and CIA are here together to get this man out."

Roberts cuts in and says, "We want to see his belongings first."

The sergeant says, "All he had on him was this bag of money. He said you traded it with him. Is that true?"

"Yes," Debbie answers.

"How do you know he didn't steal the money he originally had?"

"I'll just say this," Debbie states, "the FBI and the CIA know that none of his money came from this area."

Roberts asks, "Are you sure this is all he had on him?"

"Just the money in the bag."

"Can we see him now?" Debbie asks.

"Yes, you can see him... Set Mr. Best free..."

I step out from the jail and say, "Hello Debbie and Agent Roberts. Can I go now?"

"Yes," Debbie says, "you can go."

The sergeant tells me, "I'll be watching you, Mr. Best."

Debbie says, "I'll be watching you, too, Gunnar."

"Me, too," says Roberts.

The officer from the park walks up and asks, "What's going on? I just arrested this man and he's already getting out?"

The sergeant replies, "Ask the FBI and CIA over there."

He then hands me my bag of money.

I look at the officer who arrested me and say, "Do you want to hit me again in front of the FBI and CIA?

"It's been fun in here...

"Agent Alley, can you take me to a hotel?"

She agrees and we make our way to a hotel there in Berkeley.

Parked out in front, Debbie asks, "Can I come in with you?"

"Sure, why not."

"Me, too?" Roberts asks.

"Yes, you come in with us."

We go inside and the receptionist asks, "How many rooms?"

"Just one," Debbie replies with a smile, "the best room you've got for Mr. Best. Have the bill sent to the FBI office. Here is my card. See that he gets anything he wants, sir."

"No," Roberts says, "the CIA will pay for this man's room."

"No," Debbie tells him, "the FBI will pay."

"In any case, Mr. Best," the receptionist says, "your room is free. Please sign here." He tells the bellboy, "Take Mr. Best to his room."

"Where are your bags, sir?" the bellboy asks.

"I don't have any right now but I'll buy some clothes here today."

"Those clothes are on me!" Roberts says. "Whatever you need!"

"So long, Roberts and Debbie. I will see you later."

The bellboy drops me off at my room. It looks nice. I jump on the bed then lay down to sleep.

In the morning, I get up and go get breakfast within the hotel.

I sit at the counter where the waiter asks, "What'll it be, sir?"

"I'd like coffee and a piece of pie. Any will do as long it's pie."

The waiter acknowledges me and soon returns with my order.

"The coffee is good here," I say.

"Thank you, sir."

"Look at that pretty woman over there," I tell him.

He looks at her, too, and says, "She is very pretty. I like her."

"Not me. I love her!"

As I drink my coffee and talk, I see two men watching me from a back table. I know they're from the FBI or CIA to keep an eye on me.

The waiter asks, "Live around here?"

"No, I live a long way from here.

"I think I'll go for a walk. How much is all this?"

"One dollar and ten cents."

"I'll just sign for it. Let's see, I have to give a tip. Let's just make it for five dollars."

"Wow, thank you, sir."

"No, thank your Government."

I get up and walk outside.

Downtown, I spot those same men from the restaurant behind me. They're good but they don't know I see them.

I go into a store. I look around for a bit then go back outside.

I see a movie theater. I think I'll see a movie. I ask the woman in the ticket booth what is playing today.

"It's about The Ten Commandments."

"I've seen that movie so many times on TV," I tell her. "I own it!"

"I don't think so, sir," she says, "It just came out today."

"To you, maybe, but not for me. It's an old movie but it is a good one to watch again and again. How much?"

"Twenty-five cents, sir."

Watching that in a movie theater was an interesting experience…

Afterwards, I continue my walk downtown.

I see a pizza place. Some pizza and beer sounds good.

I head in and tell the kid behind the counter, "A small pizza with everything on it and a beer."

He says, "That will be $3.85, sir."

I pay the kid and sit down with my beer.

After a while, they eventually bring me my pizza.

As I begin to eat, a few motorcycle riders enter and look around. They come over to my table. One of them says, "You're in our table. You better get up and go."

"It's my table now," I tell him. "Go away before you get hurt."

"What did you say to me?"

"I said go away before you get hurt. You do understand English, don't you?"

The man responds, "Are you looking for trouble?"

"I'm trying to eat my pizza so go away."

Another man says, "I have a knife in my jacket and if you don't get up right now, you're gunna see some real trouble."

"You know, there was another man one time who also wanted my table—no, he was a *boy* like you—and he's a dead boy now because of it. This doesn't look very good for you."

Another man in a leather jacket is standing beside him. I ask him, "Could you count to three?"

"Why?"

"Because if he takes out his knife, by the time you count to three, he'll probably be dead."

The first man says, "There are five of us and only one of you."

"Yes, but there are people outside who will not let you hurt me."

He walks to the door and he yells out loud through the open door, "Does anybody out there care if I hurt this man eating his pizza?

"Well, there's your help—nowhere."

He pulls his knife out from his jacket.

Five men burst in, pull guns from their holsters and take aim at the knifeman. "Put down the knife or we'll open fire!"

I say to the second man, "Did you count to three like I said?"

One identifies himself with the FBI and another with the CIA.

The CIA agent asks me what I want them to do with these men.

"If they say they're sorry, let them go."

Instantly, all the men in leather jackets apologize.

I say to them, "Don't fuck with me next time. You understand?"

"Yes…" they nervously say.

"Get out."

They walk out the door in haste.

I hear their motorcycles starting up and pulling away.

I thank the agents for their help.

One says, "Just making sure you stay safe."

"Thanks all the same."

I finish eating and head back to my hotel room.

To my surprise, Debbie is waiting for me on my bed.

"Hi, Debbie. How'd you get in here?"

"I work for the FBI. We know how to get into places."

"Right. What's up?"

"I want to ask a favor of you, Gunnar."

"I know what you want, Debbie. I can see it in your eyes, like a book that wants to be opened. No need to say—you want to go to bed with me. It's okay. I understand you are a woman and women like sex too—you can have me if you really want me that bad. You do have a sexy body and I do want you, too. In fact, I've been thinking about sex with you since I first saw you, baby. I'll do it for my country."

"No, Gunnar, that's not it. I just want to go to the future with you. I have to see it for myself."

"Are you sure you don't want to go to bed with me? I'm real good if you only let me show you. I have a great body. You'd like it…"

"I'm sure that's true, but that's not what I want from you."

"I get it. You don't want my perfect body right now but later.

"Roberts wouldn't like it if I took you to the future, Debbie."

"I don't care about Agent Roberts and what he wants."

"What about your job at the FBI?"

"I spoke to my superior and he said this is my decision. But really, it's up to you, Gunnar. Please say 'Yes.' I want to meet your brother and see what happens to this world in the future."

"My friend, Jack, told me that this would happen and to say 'No.' Well, I'm sorry for this, Jack—but I will say 'Yes' this time. You can go but for only one day. I don't know why I'm doing this…"

She smiles and watches me take something out of my pocket.

"What's that?"

"I know it just looks like a couple of coins stuck together but keep it in your pocket at all times. It's called a 'revealer.' Without it, you'll instantly freeze in time. You can't go without it. It's also a lucky thing for an FBI agent like you to have. If someone fires a gun at you, you can't be harmed. Bullets will just stop an inch from your body and fall to the ground. Never take it off.

"Remember," I warn her, "this is only for one day, okay?"

"I understand."

"I can't let you see my time machine so I'll cover your eyes."

I take a cloth from my room service tray and wrap her eyes.

"I see you brought your suitcase," I say. "You knew I was going to let you go with me, didn't you?"

She chuckles.

I push my ring and the time machine appears in my room. I hold Debbie's hand and walk her into its open door. I seat her. Once inside, myself, the time machine goes invisible.

"Hold on," I tell her as we rise off the ground.

I take the craft through the hotel wall without leaving a mark.

"We're off to 2010, February 3rd, 10:00 am," I say aloud.

Chapter 10: **Out of Time**

Eventually, I see my house down below. I take the time machine down and we settle slowly to the ground in my backyard.

I get out, walk around and get her suitcases out from the back.

I then open her door and hold her hand as she steps out. I close the doors and the time machine vanishes once more.

I remove her blindfold and she looks around at a new world.

"Let's go into my house."

I take her through the back door and we find my brother watching TV in the living room.

"Hello, James," I tell him. "This is Debbie. She works for the FBI. She's going to stay here with us for a day."

"Nice to meet you, Debbie."

"Nice to meet you, James," she says while staring at the big TV.

"This is that woman you spoke to on the phone," I explain.

"Yes, I remember. You were in 1956, right?"

"That's right," she responds.

"What are you doing here?"

"I wanted to see 2010 so I asked your brother to bring me."

"Be good to her, James," I warn. "Remember, she is an FBI agent and does have a gun."

"Noted," he responds with a smile.

"Let me show you your room," I tell her.

We head upstairs and enter the guestroom.

"If you need anything, just let me know."

"Thank you, Gunnar."

About a half hour later, Debbie comes down to the living room.

"How would you like to see a movie?" I ask.

"It might be interesting to see how a theater looks in the future."

"No, I actually have hundreds of movies here in my home that we can watch anytime we want. Take a look. I think you'll like this one. This movie is about a time machine, based on an old, famous book.

"I'll make popcorn. Why don't you come and watch." She follows me to the kitchen. "See this machine? You don't have one like this in your time. I just put a bag of popcorn in and push this button."

"Wow! You have an amazing popcorn machine."

"Well, it's popping popcorn right now but it will cook all kinds of food. It cooks a lot faster than a regular oven."

She watches it pop the popcorn until it finishes. I take out the hot bag and we head back to the living room.

The movie was a good one.

She looks at my movie collection and asks, "Are all these yours?"

"Some are my brother's."

"I wish we had this in our time."

"Would you like to go to the mall and look around?" I ask.

"The mall?"

"In your time it's called 'downtown,' I suppose."

"Oh, okay. I'd like to see that."

We go out to my truck.

"I've never seen a truck like this before."

"This is my baby."

We head to the mall and look around.

"Oh, boy," she says, "do you see that man talking to himself?"

"No," I say with a laugh, "he's talking on a phone. See that thing in his ear? It lets him talk to New York or someone in this town."

"Could I get a phone like that to use in my time?"

"No, it wouldn't work there."

"But your phone did," she says.

"Yes, but my phone is not the same, Debbie."

"Women sure dress differently," she says. "I like it," she explains, "but I think ladies look nice in dresses. The skirts here are too short."

"Sure, but women look good in short skirts, too!"

"I suppose…"

"Do you want to go to San Francisco and see how it looks today?"

"Yes. I was going to ask you that."

"Cool. We'll take BART."

"BART?"

"Bay Area Rapid Transit—the train."

"Oh! Well, San Francisco here we come!"

We take BART to San Francisco and walk around the city.

"It looks the same to me but different somehow," she says. "It's hard to explain but it is San Francisco and I do like the feel of it.

"It's funny—even after all the actual time that's gone by, for me, I was just here working at the FBI in that building over there."

"I know you want to go in there, Debbie, but it wouldn't be right."

We go in one of the stores. "Let me buy you something, Debbie."

"What?"

"A calculator. It's just a machine for figuring out math problems. There are no calculators like this in 1956. This will be the only one."

The clerk asks, "Can I help you?"

"Yes, I'd like that calculator, please, for this young lady."

"That'll be $32.42."

I pay the man and hand it to Debbie.

"You'll like it. My brother has one just like it."

"If someone asks where you bought it, just tell them you got it in San Francisco. Leave out the part about 2010, okay?"

"Okay."

We walk outside and head down the street when Debbie asks me, "Do you see that old man walking toward us?"

"What about him?"

"He looks familiar."

As we get closer, he stops and looks at her with recognition.

"Do I know you, sir?" she asks.

He stares for a moment and he says, "I think so, but I can't recall from where... What's your name?"

"It's Debbie Alley."

"I did know a Debbie Alley a long, long time ago. She worked for me in that building over there, with the FBI in the '50s."

"Is your name Marcus? Is it you?" she says.

"Yes, it is."

"Don't you remember me? I told you that I wanted to go to the future with Gunnar here in 2010?"

"My God! Yes. But you never came back to us."

"How can that be?" she asks me.

"It's because you're still time traveling. Later today you'll be back home in 1956 and time will change things from then on."

"Can you do me a favor, Debbie, before you go back to our time?"

"Of course—anything."

"Let me write something down for you," he says.

We walk back into the store. Marcus sees a sales person and asks for a piece of paper and envelope. He writes something down but asks that we do not read it. He hands it to Debbie and says, "When you go back, please give me this envelope."

"I will," she tells him. "I'll see you tomorrow in 1956."

"I always liked you, Debbie," he says. "You're a good person."

He then walks way, alone.

Debbie remarks, "He's so old now. The last time I saw him he had life in him but it's not there anymore. It's like the fire went out in him somehow. Something is wrong. I can feel it…"

"You'll have to wait until 1956 to find out," I tell her.

"And that's tomorrow," she says.

"Let's head back to my house."

Once there, Debbie sees my brother at work on his computer. She says to him, "I wish I knew how to use that."

"It's not that hard," he responds. "Sit here."

Over the afternoon, my brother teaches Debbie how to use the computer. She's gotten very good at it. Better than me!

"Gunnar, could I buy one of these and take it back?"

"No," I explain, "it's not ready to be invented yet in your time and people will talk about it and change things too much."

"I'd give anything for a computer like this back in my time. There is nothing you can't do with it. You don't know how lucky you are to be living in this time and to have something like this in your home."

She turns to me with a serious face.

"Gunnar, I want to stay longer. I love it here. Please say it's okay or I'll cry in front of you."

"Ugh. I can't take it when a woman starts crying in front of me. I'm only human, you know."

"Let me hear those words out of your mouth, Gunnar. Say that I can stay a little longer. I know I belong here and not in 1956. This is my time and my home. I was just born too early!"

"You agreed to only one day, remember?"

"Yes, but that was then and this is now. I didn't know what you were going to have here. I *have* to stay longer. A day is not enough."

I think about it as I turn and leave the room.

I hear Debbie pleading with my brother. "James, please help me."

"Okay, I'll ask if you can stay another day."

"Do this for me, James, and I will love you forever!" she says.

My brother comes to me and asks, "She doesn't have to go today, does she? Just let her stay 'til tomorrow. I am asking you as a brother. One more day. Do it for her and for me."

"Okay, okay!" I shout. "One more day. But that's it and no more, do you understand me?"

Debbie pops out from the other room with a big smile on her face.

I tell her, "When I saw you yesterday in my hotel room, I looked in your eyes and I knew you were going stay longer than one day and I was right. I know women. They say one thing but mean another!"

Debbie laughs and hurries back to the computer.

An hour later, I come back to find her still there.

"Boy," she says, "you can find anything you want on a computer. You can even buy things on it. I love it!"

"It's time to eat, Debbie."

"It's hard to stop on this thing. I want to know so much but time keeps on ticking."

We go to the dining room where James is seated and waiting.

I go in the kitchen for the food. I can overhear James whispering, "It's my brother's week to cook so say it's good. After all, he did say you could stay one day longer, okay?"

We soon begin tearing into dinner when James asks, "So what do you do for the FBI, Debbie?—if I may ask."

"I work for the counterfeit department. We work together with the Secret Service to investigate counterfeiting activities in the Bay Area.

"Your brother walked in my office with money he said was from the future. I thought he was nutty. However, when I saw what money he had, I knew that nobody in my time could've made it and what he was telling us was the truth."

I say to her, "Now here you are eating dinner with us in 2010!"

After dinner, I ask Debbie, "Do you want to see another movie?"

She responds, "Yes, I would like that."

"What would you like to see?"

"I would like to see a love story."

"You'll like this one," I say. "It's about this boy who falls in love with a girl in 1940."

James says, "Instead of talking about how good it is, put it on!"

So we watch it.

Afterwards, Debbie remarks, "That *was* a good movie!"

"Well," I say, "I'm going to bed now. Tomorrow is a big day for us since you're going back to 1956."

I stop and hear Debbie say to James, "I don't want to go back yet. I love your computers, phones and microwave ovens. Computers in '56 are so big they fill a room and take so much time to do anything."

He replies, "I thought you'd be missing *me,* not my computer."

"Yes, James, I'm going to miss you, too. You know that."

"Does my brother really understand how you feel about staying?"

"Yes, he knows."

"Well, as far as I'm concerned, if you want to stay with us, your room will always be here for you—today or in the future."

"Thank you. It feels good to hear you say that."

"Well," he says, "I think I'll go to bed now. See you tomorrow."

In the morning, after breakfast, I tell Debbie, "Okay, it's time to head back to 1956."

She looks to my brother and says, "Bye, James. I'll see you some day in the future, maybe" and gives him a hug.

"Wow, I've never been hugged by an FBI agent before."

"Okay," she tells me, "let's go back now to 1956—the same time we left so nobody will know we were gone."

"I have to cover your eyes again…"

We get into the machine and are off once more to the past.

Arriving in 1956, I slowly park the craft inside my hotel room.

We get out and I close the door. The time machine vanishes.

I take off her blindfold.

She says, "Thank you so much. I shall never forget seeing all the new things that will come to be in the future."

"Debbie, don't tell anyone about the future, okay?"

"I know," she says, "but can I still give Marcus his letter?"

"I forgot about that. We did promise him. But when you tell him, I should be there with you."

"Let's just go right now and get it over with," she suggests.

We head downstairs.

I find some CIA agents there watching us.

We walk out to the car and take it to the Federal Building.

Walking in Agent Marcus' office, he quickly stands up and asks, "Where have you been? I've been looking for you all day."

"I told you I wanted to see the future," she explains.

"And?"

"Well, Gunnar took me and I saw you there. We spoke a little and you wrote something down in a letter and asked me to give it to you. Here it is, sir. You told me not to open it."

Marcus opens the letter and starts reading it.

His eyes begin to fill with tears and soon he cannot stop crying.

Debbie asks, "Can I help you, sir?"

"No," he replies, "give me a minute, Agent."

He sits down slowly and breathes deeply.

"Thank you both for this," he tells us. "It says that my wife, son and daughter will be killed on vacation next month. They die in a car accident going to the lake. I have to work that day so I don't go with them. Afterward, I live the rest of my life alone. I love them so much. They would have been gone from my life."

Marcus gets up and hugs us.

"I can stop this from happening now thanks to the both of you. You saved my family."

"Glad to help," I tell him. "I must go now. I'll see you two later."

"Where are you going?" Debbie asks.

"There's a place I want to go for a cup of coffee..."

I exit the Federal Building and catch the next bus to Berkeley.

Arriving there, I head for a particular restaurant.

Once inside, I look around and see Mary, the waitress.

"Hi, Mary. How are you doing?"

"I'm fine, Gunnar. Nice to see you again. What have you been up to since I saw you last?"

"Same old thing," I tell her. "What about you?"

"Working here every day—just making coffee and thinking about when you'll come by again."

I sense that Mary is flirting with me, but she must realize by now that I have a thing for Rose. I guess it's harmless enough. Still, Mary does have her attractive qualities, too... I am only human, after all.

"Oh," I say, "It's always nice when someone's thinking of you.

"Anyway, have you seen Rose?"

"Yes, she comes in every day and asks if I've seen you."

"Can I have a cup of your best coffee, please?"

"Sure."

We talk a little while until Rose walks in and sees us. She freezes for a moment then comes over and sits down beside me.

"How have you been, Gunnar? I haven't seen you."

"Good," I reply. "I was thinking about you so I thought I'd stop by and have a cup of coffee."

"I'm buying your coffee today, remember?"

"Yes—and knowing that you are, somehow makes it taste better."

"After I saw you last, I went home and my mother asked me why I took so long. I told her I met this man at the restaurant and we talked about all kinds of things I never thought of before.

"She asked me if you lived nearby and I told her 'No.'

"I could tell she was starting to act overly protective of me again.

"I told her I gave you my number and she was upset I did that for someone I don't know. I told her this was 1956 for crying out loud!

"She said you might be a killer and that I don't know what kind of man you are. I said that if she only knew you, she wouldn't say that."

"Well, I understand how mothers are," I tell her.

"What are you doing tonight?" she asks.

"Nothing at all. Why?"

"Because there's a nice place I want to go with you."

"What is it?"

"It's called *The Top Hat*. I know you'll like it."

I look at Mary and she looks at me. I ask, "Can Mary come, too?"

"Yes, if she wants to."

Mary says, "Can I ask a friend to come with us?"

"Sure," we respond.

"Great!" Rose shouts. "It's just around the block."

"How about I meet you there," I say. "I don't have a car."

"That's fine with me. I'll be there at eight o'clock!

"I have to go now to get my hair done for tonight…

"Here's my ten cents for your coffee, Gunnar. Bye!"

"There she goes…" I say to Mary. "Have you been there before?"

"Yes, it's a nice place."

Back at the Federal Building, Agent Roberts says to Agents Alley and Daniels, "Back at the CIA office, we don't really believe Mr. Best is a time traveler. And make no mistake, we do know everything that goes on in this country. It is my intention to find out what he is up to. If it comes to it, I'll lock him up until he tells us the truth."

Debbie says, "I believe he's been truthful with us."

Daniels says, "I always knew he was crazy! I told you all but you didn't want to believe me. Let's go pick him up."

Debbie yells, "You have no grounds to do that!"

"We're not buying his act or this story either," Roberts says.

"I believe," she says, "because I went with him to the year 2010."

"You did what?" Daniels shouts.

"I saw his world in the future. I would have stayed with him and his brother, too, if I only could have.

"Everyone had phones in their pocket. We saw films on his TV."

"So what!" Daniels says. "I watch movies on my TV, too!"

"But can you pick the movie you want to watch? He had over one hundred movies he can see anytime he wants to and can even stop the movie and go get something to eat. Can you do that on yours?

"He also had this device called a 'microwave oven.' It cooked our popcorn in just three minutes!

"So if you throw Gunnar in jail for saying he travels through time, you'll have to put me there, too!"

"Now hold on," Roberts says. "We're just talking here! You know I like Gunnar very much.

"Can you tell us what his time machine looks like?"

"No, I can't."

"You can't or you won't?" Daniels asks.

"How can you not know?" Roberts questions.

"He put a blindfold on me so I couldn't see it."

The men appear skeptical.

"They have four computers in their home!"

"You can't fit four computers into one home!" Roberts proclaims. "You should know that!"

"In *our* time, but not in the future. Theirs are small like a briefcase and very fast. Anything you want to know is right there in a second.

"The truth is, I don't want to live in our time anymore. I just love it there and hope to return and stay if Gunnar will only let me."

Daniels frowns.

"Let me show you something. This is called a 'calculator.' Gunnar got it for me. It's used to calculate math problems. Daniels, you know how large the adding machine on your desk is? This small device can do all you can do with that big machine and more."

Roberts asks her, "May I see that?" He then inspects it and says, "This works well! May I have it?"

"No, you cannot. Gunnar gave it to me, not to you."

Daniels asks, "So what are we going to do with him, then?"

Roberts responds, "Well, he hasn't broken any laws here, has he? He's free to go wherever he wants to for now."

The phone rings. Debbie answers. "Got it," she says and hangs up. "Someone's robbing the federal bank downtown."

"Let's go," Daniels says.

They rush to the bank where they find a police officer down with a gunshot wound to the leg. No one can get close enough to help him with all the gunfire erupting around them.

A bank robber is crouched behind a big truck, firing at the police.

Debbie looks to the bleeding officer and says to herself, "Gunnar, I hope you weren't kidding about this." Revealer in hand, she thinks, "My life is in your hands now."

With countless bullets spraying all around from the robber's gun, Debbie shouts to the others, "I'm going in!"

A police officer shouts, "Go back! You'll be killed!"

She walks into the street firing her handgun at the man.

He returns fire.

Unharmed, she continues heading toward the desperate gunman.

She reloads and continues her attack.

The policemen and agents watch as bullets just bounce off of her.

The gunman is finally struck and slumps to the ground.

Another man unexpectedly bursts out from the bank with another machine gun and shoots to kill.

She returns fire from the middle of the street, walking toward him.

He is struck in the chest and goes down.

Agent Alley stands there, unharmed.

She reloads again and heads into the bank.

A third man fires his automatic weapon from within.

Unstoppable, she continues in as bullets harmlessly deflect off her and onto the ground. She stands by the door and snatches the shocked robber's empty weapon pointed at her.

The police cannot believe their eyes.

"Good job, Agent," one of them remarks as the robber is removed. The rest look at her in astonishment.

She simply turns and heads back to the Federal Building.

At eight o'clock I arrive at the Top Hat and find Rose out front.

"You look like a perfect diamond," I tell her. "Your hair is lovely. You are the most beautiful woman in the world! Just look at you! My eyes cannot believe what I am seeing!"

"Thank you, Gunnar. You are so kind to me."

Here comes Mary and her friend crossing the street.

"Hi, Mary. You look quite stunning this evening."

"Thanks. This is my friend, Eric. This is Gunnar and Rose."

"Hi, everybody," he says. "Let's go in."

We enter and the hostess asks, "How many are you?"

"Four of us," Eric responds.

"Follow me, please," she says. "Here is a nice table for you."

Eric says to me, "So I hear you like to travel. I was in Mexico last week and had a great time."

"I hear Mexico is very nice," I say. "I was in Tombstone recently having a beer with a friend of mine. That's a real cowboy town."

A little man steps on stage. He yells, "I am Max The Great! I can hypnotize anybody as you will see tonight before your eyes!"

"I don't believe in hypnosis," I comment to the others.

Max calls for a few people to come onstage, including me.

"No, thank you."

Mary urges me on. "Go on, Gunnar, don't be frightened!"

"I don't believe in that, Mary."

She looks at me like I'm afraid.

"Okay," I tell her, "I'll go and you'll see it won't work on me."

"If you say so."

I walk on stage and say to the man, "I don't believe in hypnosis."

"Ah! A skeptic!" he replies. "Let's start with your name."

"It's Gunnar."

"Come here, Gunnar. Look into that light. You are feeling sleepy. You cannot keep your eyes open. You are now asleep!"

I slip into a deep state of hypnosis.

"Now, Gunnar, what do you do for fun?"

"I travel through time. I see new and old places. I go where people have never gone before in the future and the past."

Surprised, Max looks to the audience and smiles.

"Where have you been in your time traveling, Gunnar?"

"I've been to 1714, 1914, 1956 and Tombstone, Arizona in 1810."

"What did you do in Tombstone?"

"My good friend, Jack, and I were sitting and drinking beer when a cowboy came in and wanted to fight. He went for his gun but Jack pulled his gun out first and shot him. Another man went for his gun, too, so I pulled mine out and fired two shots into him."

"Are you from this time, Gunnar?"

"I am from the future. This is my past. I am from the year 2010."

"Do you like the future?" he asks as he grins at the audience.

The audience chuckles.

"Yes, it is my home."

"Where do you live, Gunnar?"

"One of my homes is on the distant planet of Antonion. They are good people there. It is too far for those of this world to travel to but I can go there in my time machine."

"You mean to say that you have been on another world?"

"Yes. They gave me a home of my own and money to live on."

"Do they have cars there on that world, Gunnar?"

"No, they use conductors."

"What is a conductor?"

"A device used to travel from one place to another in an instant."

"Can you show us how it works?"

"No, you don't have any satellites yet."

"Satellites?"

"Orbiting machines around the planet for the conductor signal to bounce off of."

"Do you have anything from the future with you?"

"My phone."

"I do not see any phone here…"

"In my pocket."

"Could I see it?"

I take it out and hand it to him.

"How does it work?"

"I can call my brother and show you."

"Does your brother live close by?"

"He lives in 2010 but I can still talk to him with this phone."

"Call your brother now," he orders. He then looks at the audience and asks, "Would you like to see us talk to someone from the future?"

"Yes… sure," they respond with some laughter.

Rose appears very uncomfortable.

I punch in my brother's number and wait for him to pick up.

"James, it's your brother."

Max puts the microphone right up to the phone.

"How is it in 2010?" I ask.

"It's raining here now. How is it in 1956?"

"It's okay."

The audience can't believe what they are witnessing. They look at me with amazement but I am hypnotized and do not see this.

"Could I talk to your brother, please?" Max asks.

I hand him my phone and he says, "Hi—James? My name is Max. I am here with your brother onstage in 1956."

Several men burst in and identify themselves as with the FBI and CIA and order Max to stop. "Wake him now!" one of them shouts.

Surprised, Max turns to me and says, "When I count from three to one and snap my fingers, you will awaken! 3... 2... 1... *snap*"

My eyes open. "What happened?"

Rose comes and says, "You were under hypnosis. You said that you are from the future. Is that true?"

"Yes, but I'm still the same person."

"I don't care if you're from the future or the past as long as you're here with me right now, Gunnar."

"Wow," Mary says, "you did say you were a time traveler before but I didn't believe you."

I then realize that I'm holding my phone. I hear my brother shout, "What's going on over there? Is everything okay?"

"I'm fine, brother. It's a long story. I'll tell you about it later when I get home. Bye."

One of the agents asks, "Could you come with us, Mr. Best?"

"Where are we going?"

"Just back to the FBI office, sir."

"Okay, just let me say 'Goodbye' to my friends here."

"We'll wait for you over there, sir." He points to the doors.

"I have to be going now, Rose. But I will come back one day. You will see." I put my arms around her then kiss her lips. It feels so good.

"Mary, you make a good cup of coffee. I will come back for more. Count on it. And I do like your name. I will always remember it."

"Let's go, sir."

I go with the agents to the Federal Building.

Debbie, Roberts and Marcus are all there in Marcus' office.

Roberts asks, "Do you know what you just did?"

"Yes. So what? I don't work for the FBI or CIA and it's my time machine, not yours. I can do whatever I want. This is still the United States of America, is it not?"

"People will talk about you, Gunnar," he says.

"What's the problem here? The FBI and CIA are good at covering things up. By morning you will have the world believing I was never here. And did I break any laws?"

"No, but if you did I could have you right now, Gunnar!" he yells.

Marcus says, "Gunnar, with what you have, there are people who would not stop until they had their hands on your time machine."

Debbie says, "You just have to be careful about what you say."

"Can I go?"

"Yes, you can go," Agent Marcus says.

"Marcus," I tell him, "take care of your family."

"I will."

Roberts shouts, "I will not hear of this! He cannot go! He has too much knowledge—too much power in his hands!"

Marcus says, "Goodbye, Gunnar."

Debbie asks, "Can I walk with you outside?"

"Sure."

When we reach the street she asks, "Will I see you again?"

"I don't know, but it's been good knowing you, Debbie..."

"Say 'Hello' to your brother for me."

She gives me a kiss and a hug. I wish it were more as I hold her.

I leave her and go to the other side of the building.

I push my ring and my time machine materializes. It rises off the ground a bit as colors glow and dance off its dazzling skin. The door starts to open and I climb inside—this time, all alone.

I look around for one last look at 1956.

I'm off again to 2010. I am going home.

Chapter 11: **Rescuing Friends**

There's my home below.

I start my descent and slowly touch down.

I get out and head inside to find my brother in the living room.

"Hi, James. What's been happening?"

"Nothing. Just reading a book."

"How was it in 1956 again?"

"Debbie's back home but she's okay there. I will miss her. It was nice having her here with us. One day maybe I'll see her again."

"She was a natural on my computer," James remarks.

"She told me to say 'Hello' to you."

"Gunnar, she does not belong there in 1956. She belongs with us. The longer she was here, the more she belonged here."

"I know that, James. But 1956 was where I found her."

"Bring her back. We have *five* bedrooms!"

"Well, I'll think about it and let you know…"

"I know what'll help you think better. Let's go to a party at Jim's house tonight! Want to go with me?"

"Sure. Jim always has lots of beer. I could use one now."

"Well get ready. It starts in an hour."

The time comes and we arrive at the party.

Jim comes out from the kitchen.

He's a good man. Everyone who knows him, likes him. He's been our friend a long, long time now.

He says, "Here's a beer for you, Gunnar, and 7UP for you, James.

"I'd like you to meet a couple of friends in from Florida. Gunnar and James, this is Larry and Ed. In six months, they'll be the first two astronauts on Mars so I thought I'd throw a party in their honor."

"Yeah," I say, "I know how it feels like to go to another planet."

Larry asks, "How do you mean?"

I then realize what I said and reply, "You know, after seeing that IMAX thing… And people always go to Mars on TV, right?"

"Yes," Larry says, "but it's different in real life, you know. You'll never know how it really feels because you're not an astronaut."

"Ah, but if you don't know me, how can you say that? What if I told you that I *have* been to another world—would you believe me?"

Larry laughs and says, "You don't have a spaceship, first of all."

"Yes, I do."

He replies, "Have another beer! It's better than any spaceship."

Ed says to me, "See that pretty woman over there?"

"Yeah."

"I like her."

"Ed," I say, "I bet if you go over there and don't tell her you're an astronaut, she'll just walk away."

"We'll see about that! Wait here and see what I can do. You might learn something."

He walks on over and says, "Hi, I'm Ed."

Sure enough, she turns and walks away from him.

He walks back and says, "You were right. How'd you know?"

"Women only come to Jim's parties with money on their minds. So if you got money, you get honey. Only then do they talk with you. It does not matter if you're a nice person or a bad person."

"Then why did you come?" Larry asks.

"Free beer.

"If I had money, I wouldn't give the women here the time of day."

Jim shouts to Ed, "Come over here, I want you to meet someone." He's standing with the woman who just rejected him.

"This is Jane. Jane, this is Ed. He's an astronaut going on the first mission to Mars in six months."

"Oh!" she says. "How does it feel to be an astronaut?"

Ed responds, "I'd love to go into it with you but I was just about to have some beer with my friend, here. Gunnar and me have a lot of drinking to do so goodbye, Jane. Nice to know you."

We walk away.

Ed and I drink and talk the night away.

"It's time to go home now," James says to me.

"Well, Ed, it has been fun. I hope you learned something about women here tonight.

"*I* learned that astronauts can drink more beer than me."

"Goodbye, Gunnar," Ed says as we depart.

For the six months leading to their mission, I had forgotten about Ed and Larry until James bursts into my bedroom while I'm napping. He shouts, "Gunnar! You have to come look at what's on TV! Those two astronauts we met at Jim's party are stranded now on Mars! They can't send a rescue ship in time so they're gunna die. They give them two days before their air runs out."

"No way." I tell him, "I won't let 'em die like dogs on that planet. I'll bring 'em home."

I go outside to my time machine and push my ring twice. My time machine appears. I get in and blast off.

I've seen Mars before, on my way to Antonion.

I fly above its surface but can't see the two men. It's a big planet. I travel back and forth in my search. I will find them in time.

I see something shiny. There they are!

I descend to their location.

I hit that button which makes my craft visible to others.

Larry and Ed cautiously approach in space suits. I open the door. Ed looks at me with shock. "Gunnar? What are you doing out here?"

"I just wanted to tell you that I'm in love with Jane from the party. I didn't want you to die before I told you that...

"Do you two wanna go back home?"

"We sure do!" Larry says.

"Hey Larry," I say, "I seem to recall you saying something about me not having a spaceship, remember? What do you say now?"

"Yes, it seems that you do have a spaceship, Gunnar."

"I'm sorry," I tell him, "I didn't hear you. What did you say?"

"Yes, Gunnar!" he shouts, "You DO have a spaceship!"

"Thank you." I say, "Yes, I do have a spaceship.

"Let's go home. You'll need to take your spacesuits off."

"We'd die!" Larry says.

"Am I dead? I have no suit on—just the t-shirt on my back. You'll be okay as long as you're within twenty-five feet of my ship. But just in case, each of you put one of these in your pocket. It'll protect you."

"But there's not enough room for the three of us," Ed says.

"We could do two things," I explain. "One of you can stay here on Mars and die while the rest of us go back home. Or, two of you can sit on that one chair together and we all go home. Just no kissing, okay? What do you want to do?"

"We'll sit together," Ed says.

Larry asks, "How long will it take us to get back to Earth?"

"I'd say half an hour or an hour, depending on you two."

"What do you mean?" Ed asks.

"It depends on how long you want to sit on the other's lap."

"The sooner the better," Larry responds.

They fit themselves into the time machine and I close the door.

Ed asks, "What's this on the dashboard?"

"Don't ask. We are going home and that is all you need to know. Just do me a favor, guys…"

"You name it," Ed says.

"When we get back, don't say anything about me."

"I don't know what the hell we'll say, but you've saved our lives," Ed tells me. "We won't say a word."

An hour later, we approach Earth.

"Can you guys see it?—Earth."

"Yes, we can," they respond.

As we enter the atmosphere, the craft burns red-hot.

Larry remarks, "You know, our country would pay a lot of money for this spaceship of yours."

"I don't need the money now. I've got twenty dollars in the bank."

I see a good place to land and set her down.

"So here we are, gentlemen—Florida! If you ever find yourselves stuck on another planet down the road, just let me know."

"Thank you again, Gunnar," Larry says.

"Bye!" I shout.

They climb out and I shut the door and pull away.

Felt good to help them.

I fly back home.

After parking in the backyard and entering the house, I find my brother in the kitchen this time, reading a book.

"Did everything go okay?"

"They are safe and sound," I report. "I do not know how they are going to explain that one, though."

"Good.

"Take a look at this book here. It covers the history of the FBI. Look—here's Debbie. She's old in this picture. She says, 'I'll miss all of my friends at the FBI but no one will know how much I miss my dearest friends, Gunnar and James Best who'll always be in my heart. They are like family to me and I only wish I could see them one more time before I die.' She says, 'before I die.' What she really means is, 'I am stuck in the past and not with you two. Please come and get me! You're the only two who can save me and make me young and happy again.' She never married, Gunnar. I think because she thought we'd come for her someday. She looks so old. I want you to go get her out of 1956 so she can be young again—or you are not my brother."

I look at her picture and can see her heavy heart.

"Okay, I'll go get her out for you, brother."

"Right now?"

"Yes, right now. Does that make you happy?"

"Yes, it does. Go."

"Can I eat first, James? Will that be okay with you?"

"Eat quickly."

After lunch, I head outside again. I push twice on my ring and my time machine appears in front of me.

I sit in the bucket seat and say, "Here we go again—back to 1956.

"You know, I think you should have a name. I think I will call you 'Nelly.' I think that's a good name for a time machine. Let's go to the year 1956, Nelly. Debbie is waiting for us there."

Through time we go again.

"There's the Federal Building, Nelly."

I set her down out front and wait for Debbie.

Eventually, I see her walking from the main entrance.

I get out and close the door.

I walk up behind her and say, "How you doing, Debbie?"

She turns to me with a look of pleasant surprise.

"Do you still want to come live in 2010 with my brother and me? Or, would you rather stay here in 1956."

"I'd love to come be with you and James if you'll have me."

"Okay, then. Shall we leave today or tomorrow?"

"Tomorrow would be better. Five o'clock? I need money from the bank and to take care of some things at home."

"Where do you want to meet?"

She writes down her address.

"Okay, I'll see you there tomorrow."

She hugs me but there is no kiss.

I go back in my time machine and enter tomorrow's date, time and location, and instantly appear in front of her home.

"You're right on time!" she says.

"Well, I did come in a time machine…"

"Let's put your stuff in and go."

"There's just one more thing I have to do—call Agent Marcus."

We go into the house and she picks up the phone and dials.

"Hello, sir, this is Agent Alley. I wanted to tell you that I'm going with Gunnar to live in the future. I will not see you again."

"Yes you will," I overhear him say. "Because I want you to come to my home in 2010, okay?"

"Yes, okay. I'll see you there. Goodbye, sir."

"Goodbye, Debbie, and good luck there."

"Let's go, Debbie."

"Don't you need to blindfold me again?"

"Nah."

After loading her things, we get in the time machine and the doors close. I pull back, then push forward on the steering wheel and we go up and straight through Debbie's home and come out the other side.

Debbie says, "There's San Francisco! It's beautiful from up here."

"I knew you would like that."

I can see our home below. I set down slowly.

We get out and walk into the house. James is there waiting for us.

"Hi Debbie," he says. "I knew you were coming back to us. I just knew it. Your room is the same as you left it.

"The only thing is that you can't use my computer anymore."

"Why not?"

"Because I bought you a new one. It's in your room right now."

"Thank you, James, so much!" She gives him a big hug.

Debbie settles into her new life and a week goes by.

She says to me, "I have to go see Agent Marcus. Shall we?"

"Do you know where he lives?"

"Yes. I looked him up on the internet."

"Why not. Let's go for a visit. He's a good guy and it's been over fifty years since I saw him last."

"Gunnar, it was a week ago."

"Right. Let's take my pickup truck."

We arrive at Marcus' home in San Francisco. Debbie looks at the house for a minute then looks at me and says, "Okay, let's go in."

We step up to the front door and push the doorbell.

Marcus opens the door and looks at Debbie and me.

"Hi, sir, it's me, Debbie. You said back in 1956 to come see you again and here we are. Do you remember?"

"Yes, I remember! You look just like you did back in 1956—like it was yesterday. I realize I don't look like I used to but I'm still the same person—just a lot older. Come in and tell me about what you've been doing since I saw you last."

We all take seats in the living room.

"Well," Debbie says, "I've only been here about a week so far."

"Of course," he responds.

"Marcus," I say, "You have a pretty home out here in the city."

"Thank you, Gunnar. But call me 'Doug.'

"You never get older, do you?" he asks.

"I do get a little older but not much."

Doug's wife walks in. "I thought I heard voices in here."

"Debbie and Gunnar, This is my wife, Gail. Gail, Debbie used to work for me at the Bureau about fifty years ago."

"No," Gail says. "You're too young."

"Oh, it's true," Debbie says. "I'm thirty-one years old and I did work for your husband in the FBI over fifty years ago."

"They traveled through time," Doug explains. "I know it's hard to believe but I was there when she left 1956 so I know it's true."

"I have to sit down for this one," Gail says.

Debbie says, "Doug, I have a favor to ask of you."

"Name it."

"I want a job again with the FBI. I realize this would be difficult since it has been fifty years since I was there last. I'll need to retrain. But I need to work."

Doug looks to his wife and says, "Honey, we'll be back in a little while. We're going to the Federal Building."

We arrive and see a man at reception. Doug says, "I'm here to see Charles Lewis, please. Tell him Doug Marcus wants to see him."

The man says, "I'll tell him, sir."

He picks up his phone and speaks for a moment.

"Go into your old office, sir. He's waiting for you."

We arrive to find a man dressed in a gray suit.

"Charles," Doug says, "I'd like you to meet Gunnar and Debbie."

"Nice to meet you," he says. "Please sit. What can I do for you?"

Doug explains, "What I'm about to say cannot leave this room."

"You have my word."

"I have known you for about forty years now, Charles. You know something about my character. Yet, you may still not believe what I am about to tell you. The fact is that Debbie used to work for me over fifty years ago here in this office."

"But she only looks about thirty years old…"

"Gunnar," Doug continues, "came to my office back in 1956 with money from 2010. He met Debbie and offered a currency exchange. She wound up returning with him to 2010 and plans to stay here. Now she wants a job here again and I'm here to see if you can arrange it."

"What did you do at the FBI back in '56?"

"I worked in the counterfeit department, sir" Debbie replies.

"You can start tomorrow morning at nine o'clock."

Doug then says, "I also have another big favor to ask of you."

Charles replies, "We've known each other a long time. Name it."

"I need you to forget about all this time travel business."

Charles laughs. "Wow. Okay, but between us, how is it done?"

"I have a time machine," I tell him.

"Can I see it?"

"I'm afraid not."

"Well, okay. I guess that's all I'll say about that."

Doug tells him, "Thank you, Charles, for your help and being my friend here."

"What are friends for, if not to help?

"Debbie, don't be late for work tomorrow."

"I won't be, sir."

We then take Doug home.

Before going into his house, Doug says to Debbie, "I never did tell Gail or my son and daughter about their car accident. I couldn't."

"But Gunnar and I know about it," Debbie says.

"Thank you."

Doug does look a lot happier now than he did the last time we saw him in 2010.

We get back home and my brother asks, "So, what happened?"

"I got my job back."

"But you could get hurt there," he says.

"No, your brother gave me something to protect me. As long as I have it, nothing can hurt me. There were a few armed men robbing a bank downtown in 1956 and the bullets just bounced off of me like popcorn. You should have seen it! I didn't believe it, myself, until it happened. My job is a little dangerous sometimes, but I love it."

"Debbie and James," I say, "I have to be going again. A week has gone by and it's time to go see a new world out there. I have to get on with *my* life now."

Debbie asks, "Where are you planning to go?"

"I'll go to Florida. I have some friends there I'd like to see again. Take care of yourself and my brother."

"But I'm used to having you here, Gunnar," she says.

"This is what I do. You know that, Debbie. I travel in that time machine of mine."

"Take care of yourself, Gunnar," James says.

I go out and push twice on my ring and my time machine appears as always. I enter and close the door.

"Let's go now, Nelly. The world is out there for us. I will go alone this time with only you."

I pull back on the steering wheel and climb up into the sky.

Chapter 12: **Gunnar, Egyptologist**

From San Francisco Bay, I fly over all the other states, until I find myself in the skies of Florida.

I set old Nelly down near a bar by the NASA complex.

I climb out and go inside the bar, hoping to run into Ed and Larry. This time, though, they don't need my help.

I see many government workers in here.

I go up to the bar and order a beer.

A man across the room says to me, "What are you doing in here?"

"Having a beer. Can't you see that?"

"This place is for Army and government personnel and astronauts. I can see you're not in the Army and I know you're not an astronaut, so get the hell out of here right now."

I can tell he has had a little too much to drink so I'm cool with it. I ask him, "Are you an astronaut?"

He says, "That's none of your business."

I reply, "The truth is, you should go because I am an astronaut and you're just an asshole."

"Did you men hear what he just said?" he yells out. "He says he's an astronaut! Ha! Let's take him outside and work him over."

Larry storms in with Ed and shouts, "But this man *is* an astronaut! You fight one of us, you fight all of us."

Ed shouts, "He's got as much right to be in here as any one of us. Nobody touches him or he is a dead man. I'm serious."

The drunk man says, "This man is not an astronaut!"

Larry looks at me in the eye and asks, "Can I tell them?"

"Why not?" I respond.

"Gunnar owns a private spaceship. He's the one who rescued us from Mars. We were going to die but he came and saved us."

The drunk man asks, "Is that really true?"

"Yes, it is," Ed tells him.

Seeing a table, I say to Larry and Ed, "Let's just go sit over there."

Leaving the confused drunk fellow, we take a seat and a waitress comes over and asks, "What can I get ya?"

I tell her, "I would like a beer—and Larry's buying."

"You got it," he says.

Ed says, "No, I'm buying his beer!"

The waitress responds with, "I'll be back with three beers."

The drunk man comes over and asks, "Can I sit with you guys?"

I say to him, "No, sir, you cannot. Sorry, but this table is for noble astronauts only. So go away."

He frowns and walks off.

Ed says, "I love your spaceship, Gunnar. How fast can it go?"

"When you see a star, you can't go there because it's too far. I can get there in about seven hours."

"At one time," Ed remarks, "I would not have believed you. But I have to say that I do believe you now.

"Just to get to the Moon takes us three days, three hours and forty nine minutes!"

The waitress arrives with our beers.

"Gunnar," Larry asks, "do you believe in UFOs?"

"Yes, I do."

"Why?" Ed inquires.

"Because some of them are my friends and I like them very much. They are good people and are really just like us. One day I'll take you two to their planet. Their women are out of this world."

Ed asks, "Are they very far away?"

"You have no spaceship that can go that far."

I notice a very pretty woman walk in and sit at the bar. "I could go for that!" I remark.

"She won't talk to you," Ed says. "I tried once before and she just told me to go away."

I tell him, "I know something about women that you don't—how to talk to them! Watch me and learn something."

I get up and I walk on over to her—real slow and cool.

She's wearing a maroon-colored dress that's a bit tight on her and a little open in front and has really nice legs to look at.

"Hello there," I say. "Let me just say this before you tell me to go away. My friend behind me said that you won't talk to me. I told him that you would. If you can just help me out here, it would mean a lot. I know they're watching us right now."

She glances over my shoulder and sees them.

"Can I buy you a beer or something?" I ask.

"Well, you can buy me one beer if you want. What's your name?"

"Gunnar. You?"

"Emily."

"Would you like to sit with us over there at that table?"

She thinks for moment. "Why not? You seem like an okay guy."

We walk over to our table and I say, "Please sit. Gentlemen, this is Emily. Emily, this is Larry and Ed."

Their eyes are wide open in disbelief.

Emily sits and says to them, "I know you two are astronauts. Ever see any UFOs out there?"

"Not me," Ed answers.

"What about you, Larry?" she asks.

"Only on TV."

"I believe there are people out there in space," she says, "What do you think, Gunnar?"

"Well, this universe is too big for just us to live in. I'm sure a lot of other things exist out there that we don't know about."

We actually end up talking through the afternoon.

"I better go now," Emily says.

"I'll walk you out," I suggest.

Outside, Emily asks me, "Would you like to go visit the Egyptian Museum tomorrow? They have lots of interesting things on display."

"Why would you think I'd want to go to an Egyptian Museum?"

"Because I work there, Gunnar, and I want to see you again."

"What time?"

"How about twelve o'clock? We can go out and eat somewhere."

"Sounds good to me."

"Okay, see you tomorrow."

"Count on it."

I go back in and say to Larry, "Looks like I have a date tomorrow. Maybe I'll get lucky…"

"You never cease to amaze me."

"Ed, it's been fun. You take care of yourself."

"Good luck, Gunnar. I hope you get lucky tomorrow."

I head out where my time machine awaits and push my ring twice. I climb inside and close the door. "Well, Nelly, time to go to work."

I crack open the book of languages. I look up "Egyptian." It seems to have different stages of language. Old Egyptian goes from about 3180-2240 B.C., Middle Egyptian is 2240-1990 B.C., Late Egyptian is about 1573-715 B.C., Demotic is 715 B.C. to A.D. 470 and Coptic is A.D. 640. Which one do I want to know?

I program them all. A light goes on for a few seconds then stops. Now I can speak, read and write in Egyptian.

I enter tomorrow's date into the dashboard and set the arrival time for 10:00 am. I begin the time jump and it's already tomorrow.

I take off for the museum. Seeing it below, I locate a place to park and push down on the steering wheel as the time machine sets down.

I change my shirt and climb out.

The craft vanishes but I know it'll come back when I call it. I walk inside the Egyptian museum where Emily is waiting for me.

"Hi, Emily. How are things?"

"Things are good.

"See that man? He works here, too. He's a jerk. He thinks nobody knows more about the Egyptians than he does."

He looks over to us and approaches.

Emily says, "Gunnar, this is Rick. Rick, this is my friend, Gunnar, I was telling to you about."

"Hello, Gunnar. Come with us and that group over there and you can learn something about the Egyptian people."

We follow him.

Rick says, "This is Professor Peter Hay. He will be conducting the tour for us today."

As the tour begins, the Professor explains, "These writings tell us that a man goes and buys some food for his family..."

I interrupt with, "Actually—if I may be so bold—it states that the man's brother buys the food for the family, Professor."

Rick says with a smile, "You don't know how to read Egyptian."

"Yes, I do. I know the language very well."

The Professor says, "Gunnar is right about what it says."

"How can that be?" Rick asks.

The Professor says to Rick, "Anybody can be wrong sometimes."

I ask Rick, "You know the Egyptian language, don't you?"

"Yes, I do."

"Good, then you know what I'm writing down here..."

He studies my piece of paper for a moment. "I don't know."

I then start saying something in Egyptian. "What did I just say?"

"I don't know."

"I said, 'The man's brother buys the food,' in Old Egyptian."

The Professor says in amazement, "Nobody has spoken in ancient Egyptian for thousands of years!"

"I can speak, write and read Egyptian like it was today's paper."

"I would like you to take a look at something," the Professor says. "Please walk over here." The group follows. "What does this say?"

"It says, 'I love you with my whole heart and you will always be my true love, forever.'"

"What you just read took five years to translate. It is so old that it could not be understood by anybody. You did it in just a few seconds. Do you want a job here at the museum?"

"No, but I do want to go out with Emily for lunch."

"Gunnar," she says, "you have to ask *me*, not the Professor!"

159

"Emily, would you like to go out to lunch with me?"

The Professor asks, "What college did you go to?"

"Just high school, Professor."

"Please, call me Peter. You are the smartest man I've ever known! I'm so happy Emily met you and that you came here to this museum."

Rick puts on a resentful face.

"I'll make you a deal," I tell Peter. "When we get back, I will read anything you want me to read. It does not matter how old. Tomorrow, though, don't ask me anything more about it."

"Okay, Gunnar. You got a deal."

"Emily, let's go eat now."

"Let me get my purse. Follow me. There's a place I like to go…"

Near the museum we locate the restaurant and go inside.

Our waiter greets us and leads us to our table.

"What would you like to drink?"

"A beer," Emily says.

"Two," I tell him.

The waiter hurries off.

"I didn't know you spoke Egyptian."

"There are a lot of things I don't know about you, too, Emily."

The waiter returns with our drinks. "Ready to order?"

Emily responds, "Two burgers with fries."

As the waiter leaves, I notice Larry entering the restaurant with a woman I do not know. I wave at him. He sees us and they come over.

"Hi Gunnar—Emily," he says, "This is my wife, Anne."

Anne is wearing a dark dress and gray coat.

"This is Gunnar," he says, "The man who saved my life on Mars."

Anne gives me a hug and says, "Thank you so much."

"Well," I tell her, "I had nothing else to do that day…

"Would you like to sit down with us?"

Larry says, "Everything's on me."

Emily asks, "So, Gunnar, you went to Mars, too? There really are a lot of things about you I don't know.

160

"Did they have to fit you for your own spacesuit?"

"No, I don't bother with spacesuits. They make me look too fat."

Anne says, "I thought you needed one to breathe there."

Larry says, "I don't know how, but he didn't need a spacesuit. He came in a spaceship, opened the doors wide open, looked around and told us we were going home. If he hadn't come when he did, we'd be dead now. Just when we thought it was all over with, there's Gunnar standing there with a big smile on his face to take us back home."

Emily looks at me and says, "You're a hero!"

"No, I just thought I'd get free beer for life if I saved them."

Larry says, "Mars is a lonely place to die. My thoughts were with my wife and children. You will always have beer on me, Gunnar."

The waiter comes with our food. We eat and talk until Emily has to go back to work. We say our goodbyes and head to the museum.

Peter is there with two other men, dressed in very nice suits.

One of them says, "I am Professor Vineyard. This is my associate, Victor. Professor Hay says that you understand the Egyptian language very well. Can you tell us how you achieved this?"

"No. Peter, why did you bring these men here?"

"It's up to you, Gunnar, if you want them to stay."

"It was just supposed to be you and me."

Peter looks to the men and says, "I'm afraid you will have to go."

Victor asks "Why?"

"Because I don't like you."

They look at each other and walk off, talking among themselves.

"Do you want my help or not?" I ask Peter.

"Yes, I do."

I tell him that he, Emily and Rick can stay if they want to.

I spend the rest of the day and night reading hundreds of pieces of ancient Egyptian text until early morning.

Rick and Emily left hours ago.

"Are you sure you don't want a position here?" Peter offers. "You have the best grasp of the Egyptian language I have ever seen."

161

"No, I like what I do—which is nothing at all."

"You have answered many questions I did not even know I had. Thank you so much."

"I have to go now," I tell him.

"I hope to see you again one day. Goodbye, Gunnar."

I go outside where my time machine is parked. I push my ring two times and it appears. I go inside and close the door. I just sit there and look around for a moment. "I need to go somewhere," I think aloud. "I need some time away from all these people here on Earth. My mind needs to rest from all this Egyptian stuff as well."

I look up and see the Moon all alone up there with no one on it.

I pull back on my steering wheel and step on the pedal.

Off to the Moon I go.

Chapter 13: **Getting Away From It All**

The size of the Moon grows quickly as I approach.

I settle down on its rocky surface.

I get out and look around.

I see the Earth far away. What a world I live in…

I sit down against a nearby rock for a long while and fall asleep.

When I awaken, I begin thinking about Jack and how I am now the time traveler. It's my job to travel to different places in time.

I would like to go back and see the Roman Empire.

I get back into my craft and set the date for 538 A.D.

I pick up the book of languages and locate the Roman language. I enter its number into the computer and a light goes on and off.

I blast off the Moon's surface. Back to Earth I go.

Rome.

I do not have proper clothes for this time period but I don't really care for their clothes anyhow.

I open the door and all the people stop moving.

Out from the trunk, I pull my loaded pistol. I get Jack's gun, too. I can kill anyone now who may stand in my way.

I close the doors and time starts up again as Nelly vanishes.

People around me start moving. They stare because I do not dress as they do. But I don't care. I feel confident with my 45s by my side.

Two soldiers stop me. One of them asks, "What is your business here in Rome, my good man?"

"I'm just looking around the city. I like what I see of it so far, sir. There's no law against that, is there?"

"No, but come with us anyway, sir."

We go inside a big building. It looks like someone lives here. One of the soldiers calls out, "Paul, are you here, sir?"

A bald man walks into the room. He is wearing what looks like a white dress to me—although I'm sure not to them.

One of the soldiers goes over and talks to him but I cannot hear.

"You are not from around here are you?" the bald man asks me.

"No, I'm just taking in the sites. Is there a problem?"

"I am Paul. What is your name?"

"My name is Gunnar Best. Nice to know you, sir."

"Where are you from?"

"I am from the United States of America."

"Is it a small country?"

"Oh, no. It is a giant country. It is the most powerful in the world. Nobody wants to fight us. They know better because they will lose."

"Sir!" he yells, "*Rome* is the most powerful country in the world! It always will be!"

"Just one American soldier can beat ten Roman soldiers in a fight to the death. That is why *we* are number one. We know how to fight."

"Take him to the amphitheater!"

They grab my arms and take me to a large, open-air building with rows of seats forming a high circle around an arena.

I see gladiators practicing with swords and daggers.

Near them are a group of ragged men and women, tied up.

They pull me out into the arena. Thousands of spectators watch.

They're all dead thousands of years in my past but don't know it.

Paul yells to the crowd, "This man says his country is number one in the world and that one of their soldiers could win a fight with ten Roman soldiers! What do you say about that?"

The audience shouts, "Kill him! Kill him!"

Paul asks me, "Are you a soldier?"

"No, but I used to be a long time ago."

"If you were once a soldier of your country then you can fight ten Roman soldiers and win the fight."

"Look, I have no interest in fighting your men. I was just visiting your beautiful city. I did not come here to kill anyone over nothing."

Paul waves his hand at the soldiers and they quickly slaughter the defenseless men and women who are tied up. The soldiers then look to me, grinning with satisfaction.

"You listen to me!" Paul yells. "You fight our soldiers or die now! Here are your sword and daggers. You will fight to the death."

If I had known they were going to kill those people, I would have used my ring to stop what was happening and save them from these vicious Romans. Too late now.

"I have old Betsy by my side so you can stick your damn sword and daggers up your ass—or your soldier's."

"You will die a fool's death out there without these."

The crowd continues to chant, "Kill him! Kill him!"

I say, "We shall see who will win this fight to the death—the old American soldier or the young Roman soldiers. Let the fight begin."

"Jack," I think to myself, "I think you would do the same..."

I am shoved forward into the big ring and the soldiers attack.

I know the Roman soldiers are badass fighters, but not today, and not with me. I pull old Betsy from her holster. "You helped me before, now do it again. You soldiers have no idea what I got here..."

I fire a shot at their feet but they only stop for a moment and look with puzzled faces at the loud sound. They resume their attack and I fire again but they don't even slow down this time.

I level old Betsy at them. A soldier raises his sword and I gun him down. But they still keep coming. I fire at another and another until all lay lifeless or wounded on the ground and reload my gun.

I yell out to the crowd, "One American soldier lives but ten brave Roman soldiers die for nothing at all because of that man over there."

I walk over to Paul and say, "My country is the best in the world. Now you know it and the world knows it, too."

"What kind of weapon is that you hold there?"

"It's called a 'gun.' In my country we fight wars with it. You with your swords could not win a war against us."

"Could I buy your gun from you?"

"A minute ago, you wanted me to die but now you want to be my friend and buy my gun? Don't make me laugh! It has been interesting here in Rome but I'm going back to my country where I belong."

As I walk away, someone fires an arrow at me and it bounces off. I draw my gun and point it at Paul and fire a single bullet at his feet.

He yells, "I don't know who did that! Believe me!"

I raise my gun to his face and say, "Goodbye, Paul. I owe this to your soldiers and the people they killed."

I shoot him and he falls dead to the ground.

I leave and no one tries to stop me.

Walking down the road, I look at the people here who lived before I was born. I see kids playing and people buying and selling. All this happened thousands of years ago, yet, we are together here now.

I push my ring twice and my time machine appears and raises off the ground. My door opens and I climb in. I look around and close it.

There is a sudden violent shaking and shifting of the Earth.

Buildings are falling down, people are running for their lives.

Yet, my time machine does not move an inch.

I can do nothing for these people but watch them call for help and scream. I say to myself, "Go home now. Your work here is done. You saw Rome of the past. They died thousands of years ago."

But I am here now and I can see them hurting and yelling.

Jack once said that when you are in someone's time, you feel the same pain they do. He was right.

I climb out and witness a building falling down onto some people. I run over to help them move the stones off. I move some bricks from a man but he is dead. I see a young girl. She is dead, too. I then locate another man underneath and work feverishly to free him.

He shouts, "That's my daughter over there!"

We work together and remove the last of the stones off the young woman and pull her out from the rubble.

Her leg is broken and she screams in agony.

The man asks, "What can we do for her?"

I know they can't do a damn thing for her here in 538 A.D.

I watch as the man cries for his daughter.

I say to him, "I can help her but you must do *everything* I say."

"I will do anything to help my daughter. Please help us!"

"Sir, you are about to see something very strange. Don't be afraid. Hold this." I hand him a revealer and slip another into his daughter's pocket. I push my ring twice and my time machine appears.

The man yells, "Oh my god help me!" and he falls to his knees.

The woman is in too much pain to really notice much.

"Help me with your daughter!" I shout. "We must get her inside!"

After doing so, I order the man to get in.

Hesitantly, he climbs in and I set the date for February 10, 2010 at 10:00 am. The door closes. The time machine raises off the ground and its wings swing out from underneath. I pull back on the steering wheel and press down on the pedal as the craft flies up to the sky.

The man is obviously frightened but there is nothing I can really do about that.

"Your daughter will be okay. Be strong for her. I know this is all very new for you both. But believe me, it's the best thing for her."

I see that the young woman is frightened, too, but really has more pain in her leg than she has fear for what is happening.

I see Florida down below and head for the museum.

I park by the entrance.

"Sir, you must stay here. I'll be right back."

He nods.

I climb out and close the door. I walk into the museum and locate Emily who is talking to Peter.

Peter sees me and asks, "Oh, how are you doing, Gunnar?"

"I'm fine but I have to talk to Emily alone right now, please."

"Very well. Nice to see you again."

"What is it, Gunnar?" she asks.

"Emily, this is very hard to explain but I need your help. A young woman has broken her leg and I must take her to a hospital."

"What's the problem? Just take her!"

"Emily, the woman is with her father. They were in an Earthquake when she broke her leg. This happened 1,500 years ago. I have a time machine. I pulled her from a fallen building. I know the doctors back then would not be able to help her so I took her here."

She pauses. "Where is she?"

"Just outside in my time machine."

"Let's go see her."

We head out to the time machine and I push on my ring one time. Everything stops moving, including Emily.

I open the door and go in. I take my book of languages and look up English. I push 1-5-6-9 and a light blinks on and off.

I go out and put a revealer in Emily's pocket. I push again on my ring and she starts moving and sees the open time machine door.

She looks inside and sees the young woman with her father.

"Oh my god," she says. "My name is Emily," she tells the father. "I am here to help you and your daughter."

"Bring your car over and we'll put them in," I tell her.

Emily leaves and returns quickly with her car.

The father and daughter appear apprehensive of it but, again, there is little I can do about that.

We drive to the emergency room and wait to be seen.

A doctor finally comes. He confirms the leg is broken and tells us, "We must take care of that right way. The father can come along but the rest of you must wait here."

About twenty minutes go by before the doctor returns and asks us, "Why are they dressed like that?"

Emily says, "They're actors. She broke her leg in rehearsal."

"Well, they should be more careful."

In the waiting room, I can see a lot of questions in Emily's eyes.

But the doctor returns with the young woman in a wheelchair. He says, "She's fine. You'll need to bring her back in thirty days so I can see how her leg is doing."

We thank the doctor and walk out to Emily's car.

I whisper to Emily, "She has to be returned to the past where she belongs, but she can't yet. What are they going to do for thirty days?"

"Just let them stay with me for god's sake!"

"I don't like this one bit," I remark. "But okay."

We drive to Emily's home and go inside. The Roman woman does good on her new crutches, which she quickly learns to use.

"Please sit down," Emily says.

"Where are we?" the man asks.

I say to him, "This is the future. The year is 2010. You and your daughter are here in Emily's home. You said you wanted me to help your daughter. She will be okay now but you must stay here until she gets well enough to go back home to your time."

"My name is Mart. My daughter is Diana."

"My name is Gunnar and this is Emily."

Emily asks them, "Are you hungry?"

"A little," Diana replies.

"Then I will make something to eat."

Mart says, "I will go bring some wood for the fire."

"That is not necessary," I say. "I will show you." I take him to the kitchen and turn one of the knobs on the stove, igniting a blue flame.

"Oh!" he says. "What is this? Fire without wood? It cannot be!"

Emily makes spaghetti in honor of our Italian guests and we eat.

Afterwards, we all go into the living room and talk a little.

Emily asks, "How do you like it here in our country so far, Mart?"

"I will always appreciate your country for helping us."

He sees a newspaper lying on the coffee table. He reads aloud, "Come for big savings this weekend at All-mart."

Emily asks, "Gunnar, how can he read that newspaper when he's from 538 A.D. Rome? What's going on here? Tell me the truth."

"Well, remember when I was reading Egyptian the other day? My time machine has a device that lets you speak any language you want, from any time period. Since Mart and his daughter were in my time machine, they can both read and write English now."

"Why didn't you tell me about this time machine and its language device before?"

"I get tired of trying to explain my business to people."

"Mart," Emily says, "I have a million questions about Rome and you and your daughter and the people that live there in that time.

"Gunnar, can I talk to the professor about this? Please say 'Yes.'"

"If you tell him, he'll then tell somebody else and that person will tell someone else…"

"The Professor would simply die if he found out that real people from 538 A.D. were here and we did not tell him."

"You're killing me here. I know it's wrong, but call him anyway."

Emily goes to the phone. "Peter? This is Emily. Can you come to my house right away?"

"I'm very busy," I overhear him say. "Can it wait 'til tomorrow?"

"Okay, but tomorrow you will just be mad at me for not insisting that you come today."

"Fine. I'll be there in a little bit. Goodbye."

The professor eventually arrives at the house where Emily and I greet him and bring him into the living room.

"What's this all about?"

"Peter," I state, "although what I am about to explain might sound unbelievable, you must agree not to tell anyone about it."

"You have my word."

"I have a time machine." I then go on to explain what happened.

Peter asks, "Can I see them?"

"They're in the kitchen," Emily says.

We lead Peter into the kitchen where I say, "Peter, this is Mart and his daughter Diana."

Mart says, "Greetings, Peter. How are you?"

"I'm fine," Peter responds. "You speak good English for Romans from the year 538 A.D."

"I'll explain that to you later," Emily says.

Peter inspects their clothes and shoes and asks, "Is this some kind of joke? It's not very funny. You had me going but I'm not buying it."

Mart asks, "Why does this man think that we are a joke?"

Emily suggests to Peter, "Maybe you better go."

I tell him, "This is no joke. These people *are* from ancient Rome."

Emily looks Peter directly in the eye and tells him, "It is the truth. I saw the time machine they came in."

The Professor carefully looks around at everyone's faces and says, "I apologize to you and your daughter."

"I understand, Peter," Mart responds.

"How long will they be here, Emily?"

"Until her leg is better—a month."

Peter says, "We should get some clothes for them to wear here."

"I have some clothes for him in my time machine."

Emily says, "I have some clothes that ought to fit her, too."

We retrieve the clothing and they put them on in the next room.

Peter says, "It's so hard to believe they're from 538 A.D."

Mart returns after a few moments, wearing his new clothes.

Peter asks him, "Can you please tell me about where you live and the people in your city?"

"I would love to."

"I'll make a pot of coffee," Emily says.

They talk for many hours into the night.

I relax in the living room and watch TV.

It's getting late.

Peter walks in with Emily and says, "I have to be going now."

She says, "I bought a house with three bedrooms so I could make extra money. I never thought I'd be using it for guests from 538 A.D."

"Emily," Peter says, "the museum will pay you for their stay here. I will see you here tomorrow. You have quite an excuse to stay home from work this time."

The Professor departs.

"Gunnar," Emily asks, "Would you mind sleeping on the couch?"

"Emily, if I hop in my time machine, thirty days will go by in two minutes. Think you can take care of Mart and Diana by yourself?"

"Yes, Peter and I can take care of them."

"Great. See you in a month."

I climb into my time machine, enter thirty days on the dashboard computer and initiate time travel. I climb out again and head back into the house as if only a moment had passed me by.

Emily greets me in the kitchen.

"How are Mart and Diana?"

"They're fine. In fact, they want to remain here in our time."

"Ah! What are you trying to do to me? They don't belong here."

Mart walks in with Diana.

I ask them, "Don't you want to go back home to Rome?"

Mart replies, "No, Gunnar, we want to live here."

"Mart, do you remember agreeing to do what I say?

"Yes, but it's so much better here than in our time."

"But it's not right this is not your time in this world. You belong back in your own time."

Peter enters the house and finds us in the kitchen.

"Peter!" I say, "Can you help here? I am trying to take these two back to Rome but they want to stay. Say something!"

"I also want them to stay here with us."

"Diana," I explain, "you could have married a nice man and had a good marriage with kids and who would have children, themselves. But if you stay here in 2010, your children would never be born."

"Father," she says, "I'm not sure what to do now."

Peter says, "I got Mart a job at the museum and he likes it there."

"Doesn't he need a Social Security card to work there?"

"I got cards for them both. I have a friend who arranged it."

"Fine. Here's my number, Diana. Goodbye to the rest of you. You people make me sick. I knew I shouldn't have gotten involved."

I go outside to where my time machine is parked and get in.

From there, I navigate back home then sit outside for a while.

I walk into my house and check my answering machine.

"It's Diana. I have been thinking about what you said. In my time, people only lived to about forty. I did not have a boyfriend back then, as you say, so I think it's better here for me and my father. Thank you for everything you have done for us. I hope I will see you again."

Well I guess that's that. She may be right. I feel a little better now.

The next morning, I go to Tom's house. Sitting in his living room, I ask, "So how's the cancer?"

"It's gone. I'd be dead by now if it weren't for you.

"If I had a complaint, it's that I'm too fat. I weigh three-hundred pounds, which is not good. I'd give anything to lose it but I just can't. In school, I was pretty thin. What happened?"

"Tom, if you really want to lose weight, I can help you. I'll come back with a solution soon. I give you my word."

I go out to my time machine and set it to go back twenty years at around seven in the morning and launch my craft back into time.

I fly over our old high school and find Tom down below. He looks so young. He's running by himself around the track.

I get out and walk to him. "Have a minute, Tom? I'd like to talk."

"I know you," he says, "but I can't remember from where…"

"I'm Gunnar Best, your best friend. I'm from the future and so a lot older now."

"Is this some kind of joke?"

"Tom, the first time I saw you, we got into a fight. As I recall, you kicked my ass… but now you are too young to kick my ass…"

"If you are Gunnar, what do you want from me?"

"Tom, I'm here to help you in your future, because I gave you my word that I would. I need your help to help you."

"What can I do to help myself?"

"I want you to go with me to the future and see yourself. But do not say who you are when you are talking to yourself, okay?"

"I don't really believe you're Gunnar, but how do we get there?"

"Hold this in your hand."

I then push my ring two times and my time machine appears.

"Oh my god! You're not joking!"

"Remember, Tom, you still owe me five dollars, too."

"Yeah, I know."

We both climb in.

We return to 2010, in front of Tom's house.

"Here, put this big hat on," I tell him.

We walk in and I shout, "Hi, Tom, it's me!"

"Come on in," he shouts back. "I'm here in the living room."

"Tom, this is a friend of mine. His name is… Tommy."

"Hello, Tommy."

Tommy just stares at his big, fat self. I know what he's thinking—"How did I get so fat?"

Tom remarks, "Don't I know you? You seem like someone from a long time ago, but I can't quite place from where…"

"Tom," I say, "I talked to someone about your weight. He said he will help you lose it. Tommy, you know that person, don't you?"

"Yes, I do."

"I'm at three hundred pounds," Tom says. "If I were young again, like you, I'd watch what I was eating, Tommy."

"I believe you."

"Tommy and I have to talk to that person who can help you, Tom. He is very close to us. He'll help, right Tommy?"

"You have my word."

Tom says, "Thank you. Tommy, you will never know what a good friend Gunnar is. One day, I hope you will find a friend just like him. What would I do without you, Gunnar?"

"What can I say?" I tell him.

We go back out to the time machine and climb in.

We don't say a word until getting to Tommy's time when he says, "You are my best friend, Gunnar. Thanks."

"Just don't forget that five dollars you owe me."

"I'll give you ten."

"Don't tell anybody about what happened here today and watch what you eat. Take care of me in your time, too."

Chapter 14: **The Men on The Moon**

I take my time machine back home where I just want to sleep.

I hit the hay and when I wake up, I go downstairs and say to my brother, "I'm going to have a barbecue today."

As I cook my burger, I hear a car pulling up in our driveway.

A ring of our doorbell soon follows.

I hear James opening the front door and greeting someone before coming out to the backyard with Ed.

"Ah, would you like a burger, Ed?" I ask. "I make a good one."

"I'll get plates!" James says as he runs back into the house.

"Gunnar, I need your help," Ed says.

"Just say the word! You want one of those women at the party?"

Debbie walks out into the backyard.

"Ed, this is Debbie. She's a friend who's living with us right now. She works for the FBI. She has a gun and everything."

"Hello, Debbie.

"Gunnar, could I speak to you alone?" he asks.

"You can say what you need to in front of any of us."

"Gunnar, I have to get to the Moon to help some fellow astronauts in trouble."

"But my hamburgers are almost ready."

"Hear him out, Gunnar," Debbie says.

"We have to go right now."

"Why?"

"Simply put, a certain critical chip on their spacecraft is damaged. Without it, those astronauts will suffocate within the hour. I need to bring a replacement and fix it. There's no time to send another craft to save them. Can you help us here?"

"Remember that party? We drank beer and became friends. I went to Mars to help you because of that, Ed. If you did not go to that party I would not have gone up to Mars to help you. I can't save the whole world—I am only one person."

"Remember the bar at NASA?" he asks.

"What about it?"

"Remember that man who wanted to fight you?"

"Sure."

"His name is Don. He's one of those men up there now and needs our help. Do you want his death on your conscience? He has a wife and kids. What are you going to do? Let him die or let him live?"

"Damn you, Ed! You know I won't let him die!"

James comes out of the house and asks, "We ready to eat?"

Debbie says, "No, James, Gunnar is going to the Moon right now. Your brother is going to save someone's life."

"Can I have your burger, then?" he asks.

I sigh and say, "So long, James and Debbie. Let's go, Ed.

"Do you still have that thing I gave you on Mars?"

"Yes, I always have it on me, Gunnar. It's my good luck piece."

I ask him, "Could you turn around for me?" and he does.

I push my ring twice and there's my time machine.

Ed turns and sees it. The doors open and it raises off the ground.

"Let's go to the Moon," I say. "You have that chip on you, too?"

"Yes—in my pocket."

He closes his door and I take us up into the sky toward the Moon.

I see Debbie and my brother down below eating my barbecue.

Soon we begin our descent to the Moon's surface.

Ed directs us to where the NASA craft is located.

I push that button which lets others see us.

I set us down. "Easy does it, old Nelly."

Through the NASA spacecraft windows, the astronauts stare at us. They're already wearing their spacesuits. I guess they really needed to stretch their oxygen supply.

"Open the door, Ed."

"But there's no air on the Moon!"

"Open the damn door, Ed! You know better than that!"

He finally opens it and we climb outside.

176

The astronauts exit their craft and walk toward us, amazed.

Ed proudly says, "Here's the chip you need, Don."

Don asks, "How are you still alive?

"And how did you get here so fast? I just spoke with NASA five minutes ago and they said you might not make it here in time."

"You *told* them?" I say to Ed.

"Nothing specific."

"Nice to see you Ed," the other astronaut says, "but can I have that chip now, please?

"And who are you?" he asks me.

Ed explains, "His name is Gunnar. You two owe him beer for life or we take that computer chip back to Earth."

"Sounds fair," he responds.

"Gunnar," Don says, "this is Roy."

Roy asks, "So how can you survive out here without spacesuits?"

"My spaceship lets me go out for twenty-five feet without any air. So don't try it around yours or you'll die.

"We have to be going now," I say. "You'll be okay now that you have that chip. I'll see you on Earth someday. Take care."

We go back into the time machine and I take us up and away.

Ed says, "Thank you, Gunnar, for helping those men out."

"It's okay, Ed. I'll get some more free beer out of it.

"What are you doing today and tomorrow?"

"Oh, I don't know. Why?" he asks.

"Do you want to go to the planet Antonion and see some aliens?"

"Really? Yeah!"

Since my language is already programmed to speak Antonion, Ed won't know what I'm about to say. I call John on my conductor phone and leave him a message on his voicemail. "John, this is Gunnar Best. I'm coming to your planet today and bringing a friend. Please do not talk about time travel while we are there. And say 'Hi' to your lovely daughters for me. I'll arrive in about one hour."

I push the autopilot button that leads to Antonion.

Ed asks, "What language were you speaking?"

"It's the language of the world we're going to."

He says, "You're pretty smart to be able to speak a language from a different planet."

"Yes, I am pretty smart. You're right about that."

"Wow," he remarks, "we're going very fast—faster than anything else on Earth can go."

"Old Nelly can do it. To get to this planet would take years with what we have on Earth."

I see the planet coming up ahead.

We enter the atmosphere and the skin of the time machine glows red hot, yet, it remains nice and cool inside.

We soon settle down as slow as a feather to the ground.

I open the door to a new world for Ed to see and we get out.

I see John ahead, coming toward us with his daughters.

"Hi, John. This is my friend, Ed. He is also from Earth. Ed, this is John and his daughters Karen and Gail."

They all exchange greetings.

John says, "Let's all go to my house."

As we walk, I see that Ed does not believe his eyes.

We arrive at the house and Ed looks around it like I once did.

John says, "Please have a seat and make yourself at home. Would you like something to drink?"

I say, "I would like one of those drinks I had last time I was here."

"Make that two, please" Ed says.

Karen goes to get them.

John says to Ed, "I hope you will like it here on Antonion."

I ask, "What happened to those men that hit me in the restaurant?"

John replies, "I thought you knew—they were sent to live on your Earth for one year so they can learn about people on other worlds and be more tolerant of them. You might even see them there someday. They can still come back when their time is up if they want to."

"So you have no jails here?" Ed asks.

"No," he answers, "but they can choose any of twenty-one worlds to stay on. One of them, of course, is Earth."

Karen arrives with our drinks. She has a good heart. You can just feel that from her.

John asks, "How long are you planning on staying, Gunnar?"

"About a day. I just want Ed to meet your people and have fun."

John says to Ed, "I hope you like it here on our world."

"I already do."

"What do you do on Earth?—if I may ask."

"I'm an astronaut. I travel to our moon and to a planet in our solar system called 'Mars.' We can't go very much farther than that in our spaceships yet but one day we will."

"Impressive," John responds.

"We better go now," I say, "but we'll be back to visit again."

I walk over to Ed and say, "Give me your hand." He gives me his hand and looks at me funny as I hold it. I take out my conductor and program it for my apartment and in a flash, there we are.

"What just happened?" he asks.

"We used the conductor to get to my place. It takes you where you want to go in no time at all. Not bad, heh?"

Ed looks around and says, "Gunnar, you have a sweet apartment. What does this cost you?"

"Actually," I tell him, "it's free for me, forever. They also give me five-thousand dollars a month for life because I am the first person to come to their world from Earth."

"This is nice furniture you have here, too. And it's a two-bedroom with a big kitchen. What more could you ask for?"

"The IRS says you have to tell them if you have money in another country but they don't say anything about another planet!

"You're about my size—in that room are some clothes that should fit. While you're getting dressed, I'll get us some dates for tonight."

I enter a number into my phone and a woman answers.

"Blanca, this is Gunnar from Earth."

179

"Oh, hi, Earthman" she says.

"I'm back in town with a friend from Earth. Would you like to go out with us this evening?"

"Yes, that sounds great."

"Could you bring a date for my friend, Ed?"

"Sure. Where would you like to go?"

"How about that place we went last time? About eight o'clock?"

"I will see you there," she says.

Ed comes out from the other room and asks, "How do I look?"

"You look fine," I tell him. "What you think of the clothes here?"

"I think they're out of this world!"

"I should mention something, Ed. Did you notice that John and his daughters spoke really good English?"

"Yeah, I did notice that. I wondered if they had been to our world or something like that."

"Well, remember in the spaceship when I was speaking to John in his language? The fact is, they talk differently than us but I will teach you how to speak their language in just one minute."

"How can I possibly learn a new language in just one minute?"

"Come with me." I take him into the next room. "Sit here." I close the door. "Push that button there. When the light goes on and off, you can then speak in their language."

"Okay, but I'm skeptical." He pushes the button. "See, nothing."

"Ed, you're speaking their language right now."

"No way!"

"Say something and listen to yourself."

"How are you doing, Gunnar? You're right!"

"Let's go," I tell him. "We'll just walk over there and take a look around this town as we go."

Walking down the street, Ed remarks, "I have never seen things like this before. The buildings—everything is different. No one would believe me if I told them about what I am seeing now."

"Well, here's the place."

"It looks like an old saloon!" he says.

We walk inside and there's Blanca and her friend.

"Hi, Blanca. This is Ed. He's from Earth, too."

"Hello, this is my friend, Sarah."

"Let's find a table and get to know each other," I suggest.

I see Toby. He notices me, too, and comes over.

"Back from Earth, I see," he remarks.

"Yes, I'm here with my friend, Ed. Ed, this is Toby."

Toby says, "Any friend of Gunnar is a friend of mine. Your drinks are all free here today."

"No, I drank too much last time to do that to you again. I will pay for my drinks this time if that's okay with you."

"If it makes you feel better, Earthman."

He calls the waitress over to our table before he leaves. She asks what we would like to drink and I request four of their best beers.

"So what do you think of Antonion so far, Ed?" I ask.

"I do like it. It's very nice and peaceful."

Blanca asks him, "What do you do on Earth?"

"I'm an astronaut."

Sarah asks, "What do you do as an Astronaut?"

"We travel off our planet to places like our moon, look around and collect rocks to take back to earth."

"What for?" Blanca asks.

"I really don't know," he responds with a laugh.

The band begins playing.

Ed asks, "Sarah, would you like to dance?"

"Yes, I would like that very much."

As they get up, I say to Blanca, "How about you?"

"Sure, Earthman."

I did not know Ed could dance like that. He looks so happy out here on this planet—like he belongs here.

When the song ends Blanca and I return to our table. Ed and Sarah remain together on the dance floor until the music starts up again.

Blanca remarks, "I missed you when you went back to Earth. You did not say 'Goodbye' to me. You just left and that bothered me a lot. You did not know that, did you?"

"I'll always be your friend until the day I die. Please forgive me."

"I will forgive you this time but don't do it again."

Ed finally comes back to our table. He whispers to me, "Sarah and I are going back to her place. I'll see you later, okay?"

"Okay. Here's my conductor. Just push this button here and you'll be taken back to my home, okay?

"See you later, man," he says with a grin.

Blanca and I stay and talk.

Chad walks into the bar. He sees me, walks over to us and says, "Hi, Gunnar, how are you? See, I remember your name, Earthman."

"Yes, you did, Chad. You have a good memory. Do you want to go at it with the guns again?"

"No. I know you're too fast for me."

"Sit down," I say, "and have a beer with us."

"For a bit. It's not every day I get to drink with a human being."

"You know, I do have a friend with me this time, but he just left. He's not fast with a gun like you are, though. I think you could win a gunfight with this Earthman. You'll see him in time."

The two young cowgirls we met last time come to our table. I say to one of them, "Hello, Claudia."

"Hello, Earthman. How are you doing?"

The other girl says, "I would like a hug from the human. Is it okay with you, Earthman?"

I look at Blanca. I can tell she is getting a bit ticked off but I say 'Okay' anyway because I can't say 'No' to a woman wanting a hug. She feels quite good in my arms. Boy, she is hot. If I could only take her back to my apartment for an hour or two—but Blanca would not appreciate that so I better let it go. Damn it.

"Can me and my friend sit with you, Earthman?" Claudia asks.

"For a little while, but I am here with Blanca."

The waitress comes and I order five beers and pay.

Chad asks me, "What do you like about this planet of ours?"

"The women here are so beautiful. When I look around, I think I'm in heaven. If I took just one of these women back to my world, all the men would fight over her. 'Eat your heart out!' I say to them."

Claudia says, "I'll go to your planet with you and be your woman if you want me to, Gunnar!"

"Claudia," I ask, "what happened to your boyfriend?"

"He went for another woman—just like that and he's gone. So I'm free now. I'd like to try someone from another planet next. I'd like to try a human being."

I look at Blanca and can see her getting angry.

Still, I'd love to take this woman back to my planet. But John did tell me that people will be talking about me for a long time. I would love to say 'Who cares! This woman is hot! Let's go!' but I did say I would be good. God help me now! It's so hard to say 'No' sometimes.

"I'm sure any man on my world would love to have you. But I'm here with Blanca. We can still be friends, though."

Chad says, "What about me, Claudia?"

"No, I want an Earthman. I want someone out of this world."

"Gunnar," she says, "I will do anything for you if you take me to your planet."

Holy Jesus, help me here! What a body this woman has!

"I think it's time to go," I say. "What do you say, Blanca?"

"Yes, it's definitely time to go."

"See you later, Chad."

"Goodbye, Earthman. I wish I was you…"

"I gave my conductor to Ed," I explain to Blanca.

"Hold my hand."

We instantly appear at her home.

"Gunnar, I know I am the woman for you. I can make you feel so happy if you only let me prove it to you."

I give in to her this time. I'll let your imagination fill in the rest.

What a night!

In fact, I stick around for several more!

Eventually, though, I grow homesick and decide to return home.

I say my farewells to Blanca and then John.

I barely saw Ed the entire time I was here. When he does show up, I tell him, "It's time to head back home to our big, blue planet."

"I'd like to stay."

"For how long?"

"Forever! I think I'm falling for Sarah and getting far away from Earth was half the reason I became an astronaut. Can't I stay and live in your apartment? You're only here when you visit anyway."

"What is it with you people? Doesn't anyone actually like where they come from? Fine. Do what you want. I'm tired of arguing about this sort of thing. I'll catch you on my next visit. Good luck, Ed."

"Right on, Gunnar!"

Returning to my time machine, I program it for my return and go.

Chapter 15: **Crossroads**

On my long journey, I finally see Earth in the far distance.

Suddenly, there's an explosion! I must have blown an engine!

I grab hold of the controls and attempt to regain control.

There is another explosion beside me. No, I'm being attacked!

I look behind me and see a large ship. These must be the Gettion that John warned me about.

Damn! I never turned off the visibility switch after the Moon! I try switching it back on but it seems to be damaged.

Between the two bucket seats is that box John spoke of. It has two levers that look like emergency brakes. At the end of each is a button. The closest one to me fires laser bullets that should go through four-inch steel. The other launches a laser-guided bomb.

I pull up on my steering wheel and try several evasive maneuvers. I dodge a few more shots and manage to position myself to fire back. I shoot hundreds of laser bursts but they seem to have little effect. I go around for another pass. This time, I fire a laser-guided bomb. It drifts slowly toward the Gettion warship, following its every move. There is finally a huge blue explosion upon impact.

When it clears, it doesn't appear to have done anything!

I could just open the door and stop time but who knows if that still works with all this damage. I better not risk it here in outer space.

Quickly, I program Nelly for the random date of January 10, 3009 at 10:00 am. I pull back on the steering wheel and I step on the pedal.

I could care less about my destination at his point.

My engines fire and the time warp pulls me out of danger.

Below me, on Earth, I see an enormous hole. Near it is a building.

I set down next to the building.

I wonder if the Gettion did this…

I get out and look over the damage to my craft. Seems not too bad. I'm sure I'll wake up tomorrow and it'll be fixed up.

I walk inside of what turns out to be a restaurant.

I ask a man there, "Where is this and what happened here, sir?"

He replies, "Oklahoma. We're in the town of—well, a meteor hit it last year and so the town is no more. They never knew what hit 'em.

"Would you like something to eat?"

"Yes, I'll have a hamburger, fries and a beer."

Afterwards, I head out and decide to come back and see this town before the meteor destroyed it. I program Nelly for January 10, 3008, 10:00 am. Time flies backward. Seasons change. People come and go. Soon enough, a whole year has rewound.

I get out and walk around this soon-to-be-extinct town.

I see a store and go in. A man there asks, "What do you want?"

"I want to buy a camera."

"Well, pick one and get out of here."

I pay the man in gold and walk outside.

Strange, how he acted…

I take several pictures of the area and the people who live here. They all look at me like I'm the most annoying person they ever saw.

I see a bar down the street. I think that's where the meteor hit—right in the middle of town. I think I'll get myself a beer there.

I go in, take some more pictures and sit down.

A man comes to my table and asks, "What do you want?"

"I'll have a beer, sir."

He replies, "We're out of beer."

Over at the bar, I watch as the bartender pours beer for a man.

"What about that?"

"That beer is for people who live in this town."

"This is not right!"

Nobody says a word or cares.

"I never want to see this town again!—which is fine because I've taken some pictures. That way after the meteor destroys it, I'll still have something to remember you all by.

"By the way, I already had a beer before I came. I just wanted to tell my friends that I drank here before it was all destroyed this town."

The man asks, "When is this meteor of yours supposed to hit?"

"I'm not going to say. Why? I want all of you good people to be here when it hits! You have it coming."

"I don't believe you."

"Frankly, I don't care if you believe me. It's still coming and you will all be dead. And it couldn't happen to a better group of people!"

I storm out and into my time machine.

I program it for home and fire the engines.

Before I know it, I'm over familiar surroundings.

Yet, I feel strangely empty.

Maybe I do just need another beer.

I take Nelly into San Francisco and set her down near a bar.

Sitting in my time machine, I look around at all the frozen people, feeling depressed.

Oh my god! There's Jack!

He's with is a very beautiful woman…

He looks so happy—much happier than I feel right now.

Here I am in a time machine, with the power to go anywhere and do anything. But all that ever happens to me is people want to kill me, kick my ass, take what's mine or use me to help them.

Maybe Jack got it right. I thought he was a fool for giving me this time machine. Now I'm wondering if he was the smart one. Maybe I ought to settle down, too. I've met plenty of women in my travels…

Which should I choose? Blanca at Antonion? Rose back in 1956? Clara in 1914? Emily in Florida? Debbie in 2010? Perhaps a new one.

"Jack," I say aloud, "this is the best lesson you've taught me yet."

Time starts moving again.

Jack suddenly finds a twenty dollar bill from 1914 in his hand.

He stops, looks around and smiles. I think he knows I'm out there somewhere watching him.

I look to the sky. That's where my time machine should be.

"Let's go, Nelly. Time is waiting for us."

I pull back on my steering wheel. Up and away we go…

www.ingramcontent.com/pod-product-compliance
Lightning Source LLC
Chambersburg PA
CBHW020610250626
47154CB00004B/1451